# My Father's Endless Universe
## by Robert E. Mitchell

The contents of this work, including, but not limited to, the accuracy of events, people, and places depicted; opinions expressed; permission to use previously published materials included; and any advice given or actions advocated are solely the responsibility of the author, who assumes all liability for said work and indemnifies the publisher against any claims stemming from publication of the work.

All Rights Reserved
Copyright © 2020 by Robert E. Mitchell

No part of this book may be reproduced or transmitted, downloaded, distributed, reverse engineered, or stored in or introduced into any information storage and retrieval system, in any form or by any means, including photocopying and recording, whether electronic or mechanical, now known or hereinafter invented without permission in writing from the publisher.

Dorrance Publishing Co
585 Alpha Drive
Pittsburgh, PA 15238
Visit our website at *www.dorrancebookstore.com*

ISBN: 978-1-6453-0897-3
eISBN: 978-1-6453-0346-6

## Foreword

I believe God sometimes uses phylogeny. He lets us think we did it, but and if we brag about it, in the climax, we will not be able to handle the consequences. When we look for God, He does not appear where we do not look for Him. The same when reading His Word; we read but don't see. To see, we must study the right books. The books Satan hasn't had his hands on.

There are many truths removed from the original Word of God. Ungodly men of yester years have put garbage in place of what was written by the Apostles. I know for sure you would never go to a garbage can for a slice of bread for yourself or family? Watch out; some books are full of garbage, God said, don't touch it (Gen, 3:3). This book is not confined only to those who take their relationship with God seriously, but also to those who are week in their faith. At a time when things look black as night, it's time to find why you are in need of something you cannot see. You may need a book like this one, or help from a man who has the mind of Christ. He is the only one available without reservation. If you read Matthew 6:7, do not use vain repetitions prayers. The so-called Lord's Prayer, a vain repetition prayer, is not for Christians; it will be for the Jews in the Tribulation. If you really study it, you will see it is to be used in the Tribulation. Does it matter what God thinks or what you think? He said, "Do not pray like the pagans do." They say the same words over and over. *(Father God, help Betty Father God, Heavenly Father, She needs You Holy Father, Father God oh Heavenly Father please Father God. And so on and on.* God does not hear or listen to this kind of gibing.

The people in this novel use prayer as a tool that God puts into action. Every prayer that gets to the Throne of God is never bypassed. Yeshua intercedes for us in heaven; the Holy Spirit intercedes for us on earth, and the Saints should do their best to carry intersession to all humanity, for everyone's sake. In Matthew 10:38, Yeshua said, "those who do not follow Me is not worthy of Me." If you do not, be ready to die the most ignominious death ever thought up. This may sound like fiction but, it is true because God said it.

The church is either the masterpiece of Satan or the masterpiece of God Almighty. If the Church is the masterpiece of God Almighty, we ought to show it so. Satan's masterpiece, his Temples of Doom, are all over the world. The good she has done is covered with a blanket of evil. Since this is true, how can she be loyal and devoted to Christ?

The Godly growth of a nation depends as much upon the vigilance of its Christians as upon its Christians leaders. We plant a garden, the crop begins to grow, yielding good produce. If we let the weeds (*evil*) grow and not water (*without God*) we become slaves to ungodly rulers and Satan himself. Get and study the truth, regardless who objects. My Bible says protect it, even with your life if need be.

**Careah and the Barley Seed**
If Careah had not taken a present (*a wan of barley*) for Yeshua when He was two years old, these two books would never have been written!

# My Father's Endless Universe

There is a well-advertised wedding near Capper Galilee. The Governor, Yeshua's disciples, and their families, best friends of the bridegroom, were present. Careah and Kedar had to wear special robes to hide their wings to attend the wedding. They looked like they were slightly humpbacked. Their friends Belcantos, Sitts, King Flash, and Queen Adore also were invited to attend the wedding of Yeshua's youngest stepsister Esther. Her other two sisters were married to wealthy men. Sarah lived in luxury. Ruth also lived a luxuriousness life. His stepbrothers Jude, James, Simon, and Joseph took over their father's business. Yeshua taught them the trade of making furniture and upholstered furniture that is very lucrative. Their father died several years ago. He had given his wife a wedding present of priceless coins. She lost one of the coins, crying her eyes out, and called her friends to help find it. After an hour or so, it was found. She rejoiced and gave a party. Her husband could divorce her, thinking she gave it to another lover. No one could take the coins, not even for a debit. Esther's new father-in-law went to Mary and apologized, expressing regret for running out of wine.

She said, "No problem, I'll talk to my son; he will solve your problem."

Yeshua had done many other miracles. She privately went to her son Yeshua stating Esther's father-in-law has no more wine.

He said, "Mother I wish you would not be telling people I can do miracles! I'm about ready to do my Father's will." He told the servants to fill six water-pots with water. The servants filled six water-pots with water and watched the water turn to 162 gallons of wine. (*That is three 50-gallon drums plus 12 gallons of wine.*)

The Governor wanted to know why this *tee-roshe* good wine was served after the *shaw-kar* strong -wine: "It's the best wine I have ever tasted in my whole life. I know good wine when I taste good wine. Who made it? I want to buy a couple gallons."

Did Yeshua ask the servants not to tell how the water became wine?

Careah whispered to her husband, "I just got a cold chill, I think an evil spirit is present. I'm going to tell Yeshua about how I feel." She had to wait until Yeshua would be alone.

King Flash turned to La'no, whispered, "That fellow wearing a black tunic has a sword under his left arm."

"If you are right, we stick close to him in case he is about to do something stupid."

Kedar mossed over to Flash and La'no, "What are you two whispering about?"

La'no whispered, "Just watch, we think there's going to be trouble. It's more than luck we brought our Lazar pistols with us. Oh, oh he's giving us an evil eye."

Flash said in a low voice, "We go to the table and get a glass of wine. He'll forget us. I really do believe he is a sinister person."

"Watch it, watch it," whispered Kedar. "He's moving toward Esther."

Flash said, "Okay, if his hand comes out with the sword, zap it. Then as fast as we can, hide our Lazars, Yeshua may not want people know who we are."

Kedar uttered under his breath, "Sure enough, he is moving toward Esther and his hand is going for his sword."

*Zap, zap!*

Both were out of sight before anyone saw what happened. The sword got so hot, the jerk dropped it. Unaware, Esther's brothers had been watching the fellow whose name was Manoah a Danite, who tried to date Esther several times. She would have nothing to do with him. He had strong alcohol on his breath disguised with garlic. They took Manoah outside. Who knows what happened to Manoah. Yeshua smiled and winked at his friends. He went over to His friends.

"I thank all of you, and you all are welcome, you people are my best friends. I love you all. Please come anytime."

After leaving the shindig, they saw Manoah lying face down, his sword twisted by his side. Eli suggested they put him in the Course and take him far away.

King Flash remarked, "I know the very place. It's the Hittite country. Most of them are 35 feet tall cannibals."

Eli sided with Flash, "It will be dark when we get there, and he can hide or run for his life."

Wonder replied, "That is harsh to do that, but he was going to kill Yeshua's sister."

"Yawl, look at those two. They must be at least 35 feet tall." The two giants were walking away from the Courser. He stopped the Courser. "Look at their hands, they're at least two feet wide."

Tara and Won both shivered yelled, "Let's get out of here. We don't want to be eaten by those two freaks, or any other wackos."

Eli said, "They don't do any farming; they just eat human flesh. They eat their enemies, and their own people. My guess is humans must have greens or will soon die."

King Flash replied, "That is a fact."

As they were leaving, Careah moaned, "Darn it, I wanted to know what Yeshua meant saying, 'In my Father's Endless Universe are many Worlds.' I think I know but I want to be sure."

Tara asked, "What do you think He meant?"

Careah replied, "We will wait till we see Him the next time we meet."

Wonder teased, "Ah come on, Careah, tell us what you think Yeshua meant."

"Well, don't make fun of me if I'm wrong. I think Yeshua meant there will be special people who go to heaven and will be given the privilege of choosing a galaxy to rule as they want to. That would be the reason He created a myriad of galaxies."

"You know what, Careah, you have to be right," beamed both Tara and Won. "The next time we see Yeshua, we'll ask Him about the galaxies."

La'no found out through the grape vine Yeshua was going to be at the Temple in the city of David. Only men were permitted in the part Yeshua was going to be in.

"Kadar, you have to work on the controls of the space ships; there may be trouble at the temple, and your wing might give you away, we can't have that. Someone might think you were some kind of freak, no insult intended. Also make sure the ladies check the Dinner Vacuum Press is working properly. We don't want to be out in space and have spoiled food. Canned food is too heavy. We need to be light as possible.

"I'm taking the Ekistic, It will hold all of us, and obeys my voice, we may need it fast in a mergency."

They headed for the City of David, and landed behind the Temple.

"There's, Yeshua going into the temple. He looks very angry, has a whip, and is heading to the people selling oxen and sheep."

Yeshua made good use of the whip, striking where it was doing best, men running for their lives, oxen and sheep becoming very excited, running in every direction and discharging droppings. What a mess for someone to clean up.

"Oh, oh! He is turning the tables over. Jumpin' Joshaphat! Those tables are solid stone, 12 inches thick, six feet wide, 12 feet long… each table has to be 20 tons each! Man, He doesn't need us, let's head home. We will see Him later."

Everyone agreed.

As they were leaving, the Jews came to Yeshua, "Show us a sign where you got the authority to do what you did."

What kind of sign did they want? He just turned over 20-ton tables. Then He pointed to His body saying, "Destroy this Temple, and I will raise it up in three days."

They answered, "It took 46 years to build the temple. How can you do it in three days?"

Some of the Jews in the background whispered, *He is some kind of a nut.*

La'no asked Yeshua if He wanted to go with them for a ride in his Courser. He replied, "I have a date with Nicodemus, maybe the next time."

Nicodemus, the head of the Pharisee council, came to Yeshua's home at night, and they became friends. He asked Yeshua how to get to heaven. Yeshua said, "You must be born again."

He said, "I am old. How can I enter my mother's womb again?"

"No, it's not that way. You must be born of the Spirit."

Nicodemus replied, "I'm confused, I know a gentile is born again when he becomes a Jew, which I am not. And when a person is crowned a king, which I cannot because I am not of the tribe of Juda. As a boy of 13 years old, I became bar mitzvah, I was born again. When I was married, I was born again. When I became a Rabbi, I was born again. When I became the head of the rabbinical school, I was born again. Now that is six different ways to be born again. I know of no other way to be born again."

"Now, Nicodemus, to be born again is how you become a Christian. A Christian is one whom God, my Father dwells. I am the Savior of the World, no other name is known among any in heaven or upon earth by which men can have salvation. I have revealed salvation through my teaching by my deeds, by my life, by my death that soon will be a fact. Then by my resurrection.

Now, Nicodemus, my friend, do you believe this?"

"Yes, I really do Yeshua."

"Then you are born again into the family of my Father."

"Thank you, Yeshua, thank you, I really thank you from the bottom of my heart. I will be in heaven, yea-hoo."

Kedar was watching T.V.

He yelled, "Hey, some guy is dunking people in the water."

La'no looked at the T.V.

"That is John the Baptizer."

Kedar questioned, "What is he doing that for? Can't they bathe themselves? Oh, look, now he is doing it to Yeshua."

La'no answered, "John and Yeshua are cousins. Water baptism doesn't save, it shows you are united with Christ."

Kedar snapped back with a smile, "I think water baptism will save if you are held under long enough."

Careah shot back, "You have to live with it."

La'no, Flash, Kedar landed behind a large knoll close to Yeshua's home. The door opened as they got close. Yeshua greeted them with a wide smile. La'no asked Yeshua if He would like to go for a ride around the world.

"Yes, I would, but first I must go to Samaria, then I can go with you fellows. Give me a week; I'll be ready by then."

Yeshua went to Samara Sychar; Jacob had dug a well close by. At noon, a young woman came to get water. Sychar had water, for some reason she came here to get water. She had no veil over her face. Married women had to cover their face. If they did not cover their face, it was death. Yeshua ask her for a drink.

She remarked, "You are a Jew, and Jews have no dealings with Samaritans."

He said, "The water you give me, I will thirst again, I will give you water to drink and you will never thirst again."

"Sir, you have nothing to draw water up, the well is 105 feet deep and 15 feet of cold water. Are you greater than our Father Jacob?"

"Like I said, the water I give, you will never thirst, you will have everlasting life." Then He asked, "I would like you to go call your *andra* human husband?"

She replied, "Sir, I have no *andra* human husband."

Yeshua said, "Yes, truly, I know you have no *andra* human husband." Then He replied, "But you did have 5 *aner.* idoles you call your husbands. Their names are *Succoth-be-noth, Nergal, Ashim, Nebhaz, Tarta,*. These are all idoles you people call your husbands. The *aner husband* idole you have now is not yours. The *aner-idole* shape of a man you worship as my Father; He isn't yours any more. Starting now, you must worship Him in Spirit and in truth. You do not have to go to Jerusalem to worship Him. You can worship Him anywhere you choose."

She said, "I know the Messiah is coming who is called Christ."

Yeshua smiling said, "I am He that is talking to you."

"Really you are the Christ?" She dropped her water pot ran into the city. She excitedly said, "I met the Messiah at the well, and He told me everything we did."

Men and women ran to the well and talked to Yeshua, and they believed. The disciples showed up; they could not fathom Yeshua talking to Samaritans let alone talking to a woman. The Samaritans invited Yeshua to stay with them. He and His disciples stayed two days. I wonder how the disciples felt staying with the Samaritans for two days The Samaritans were His first converts. Yeshua had a great feeling in his heart. It's great having people believe in God, His Father.

The week was up and Yeshua was ready. La'no landed behind Yeshua's home. La'no saw a woman standing beside Yeshua. La'no opened the ship's door. Yeshua asked, "Can a woman go with us? She is my friend. Her name is Mary Magdalene, but I call her by a nick name, Mar'ee."

Everyone in the ship yelled, "Yes, yes, come in!"

All the ladies yelled, "Surprise!" Careah, Won, Tara, Queen Adore said, "You are more than welcome."

All were introduced and hugged Mar'ee. Taking off headed west, there was a huge T.V. screen showing the sights ahead. Going over Egypt, Yeshua asked La'no to hover for a few minutes. He said, "Every one accused Moses for not going north through the land of Philistines. They had a wall 100 feet high built from the Great Sea, down to the Red Sea, with deadly watch towers 100 feet apart. The wall was called the Way of Shur. Now there is the crossing in the Red Sea. The Israelites had no weapons to protect themselves. I had Moses to stay, dead bodies would soon rise with weapons. Need I say more? Okay, let's move on."

Flying west over the Great Sea approached the Pillars of Hercules; He said, "That is where Jonah was tossed into the sea. Remember he said he went down to the mountains. This is the only place I created mountains in the sea. I had a fish near to take him to Joppa. You know the rest of his trip."

Crossing a great ocean, they came to a land of Red people. He said, "They are descendants of Shem and Japheth; they worship me as the Great Spirit." Then flying over an island, a volcano spewing hot lava, Yeshua's voice changed to almost to a whisper, "The place is like a paradise but the people living there are cannibals."

They continued crossing the blue sea to a land of yellow people, fighting each other. One tribe took egg whites and other adhesives put the glue mixture on their outer eyes lids pulling the skin up, over time their eyes grew slanted. They believed this would frighten their enemies. Yeshua asked La'no to fly two miles up into the atmosphere.

"Yes, Sir, I sure will." The ship was pressurized. Yeshua said, "Now I want you all to see what is ahead. See the dead tree stumps, limbs, stones, gravel, fish, and animal skeletons?"

Everyone was puzzled asked, "How did that stuff get up here?"

"When Noah was in the Ark, it began to rain, the water in the earth burst forth with such powerful destructive force, sending all of that debris up here. The earth was pushed off its axis; now it moves back and forth, causing four seasons. It also rocks back and forth every six hours causing tides. It's not the moon causing tide. Some people believe anything they don't understand. Oh, by the way, Noah took Adam and Eve's remains with him on the Ark."

"Really? Why did he do that?" everyone asked.

"I had him do that for a special reason, you will see and know why later."

After landing La'no remarked, "I thought we took you for a ride. You took us on one of the most enlightening rides, we will remember for a lifetime."

"Before you go home, would you all like to go to the Temple with me? You can get clothing at my home. We will be in women's court next to the treasure. Mar'ee will take you there."

La'no replied, "I know we all would love to go with you. When do you want us to go there?"

"Tomorrow."

It was the Sabbath. Yeshua was standing with His back to the treasure, talking to a lame man when several Scribes and Pharisees carried a woman in where Yeshua was, setting her down in front of Him, boasting, "Teacher, WE caught this woman in adultery." They didn't care about the woman; they wanted to condemn Him on his decision. Yeshua thought to himself, *Where is the man?* "The law says she should be stoned, what do you say?"

He stooped down, and with His finger began to scarf (engrave) on solid, smooth, colored marble. When He was finished, He had written, (*Jeremiah 17:3; They sinned carrying the woman on the Sabbath braking the law.*) "He that is without sin among you, you cast the first stone at her."

They saw and heard His finger making the sound zzzz-zzzzz-zzzz and dust flying. The jackals ran around the corner then stuck their heads out peeking watching what Yeshua was doing. When Yeshua looked up, saw no one.

He asked the woman, "Where are your accuser?"

"There is no one Lord."

"Neither do I accuse you, go, and sin no more."

His friends stood staring at Yeshua in wonderment.

Mar'ee turned to her new friends and put her hand to her mouth.

"Would you like to hear about other times God used finger to wright on stone?"

They all answered yes.

"When God gave Moses the Ten Commandments, He scarfed them with His finger. You have to believe this, too, when Belshazzar, King of Babylon gave a party for his lords, they drank wine using vessels taken from the temple of God, a huge hand appeared, and its finger wrote on the plastered wall."

Yeshua, smiling, replied, "She is absolutely right. I did do those finger writings."

They all looked at Mar'ee, then at Yeshua.

"For sure you are God's Son; there's no doubt about it."

One of the biggest mysterious mysteries of all time, why didn't Yeshua go to John the Baptist's aid? John did no wrong; he only told Herod the truth. Herod took his brother's wife and all the evils he had done. He would have killed John, but was afraid of the people who believed John was a prophet. It was Herod's birthday, and Herodias had a devious scheme; to get John killed, she had her daughter dance a sexual dance to entice Herod. He was so enticed because of his muddy mind, he promised her anything she wanted. She went to her she-witch of a mother to help her decide on what to ask for. Her mother had help from the pits of Hell. What to ask for? No one on this side of Hell knew how evil a person can be. God haters are close. She will have all of eternity to suffer for her choice.

Will people clap and cheer, when God points to the gates of Hell and says enter? Will she be sorry for what she did? She will remember all eternity seeing John's head on a platter. She got what she wanted. Will she beg God for mercy? She will curse God for ever and ever.

Careah got up early, feeling great.

She said, "Kedar I feel so great if I had a place to stand I'd move the world."

He replied, "I'm glad you don't have a place to stand. I like it right where it is."

She said, "It's early, but what do you want for breakfast?"

"I'm so hungry I could eat a mule."

"Well if I served you mule, you would complain it was tough. So, you get toast, eggs, and hot tea. After we eat, I'm going to see the kids."

An hour later, she was in their air-car when a voice said, "Land." She looked around; no one was in the car; the radio wasn't on. The voice replied again, "I said land. I mean now, please."

Careah thought to herself, *Someone is playing a joke on me.*

The voice sounded again, "If you don't land, I'll land the car myself."

She landed and called her husband and told him what happened.

Kedar said "I'll call La'no, and I'll be there as fast as my air-car can get there."

La'no was there before Kedar. La'no asked Careah to get in the air-car and start the car. The air-car refused to start. La'no lifted the hood; it was only a second. He asked, "What made you land?"

She replied, "A voice told me."

He said, "That voice saved your life; the main diode is burned out."

She said, "I had a dream last night. In the dream, I was told to check on your children. That was why I was going to check on them."

La'no asked, "In the dream, were you told to check your children or our children?"

"No, I'm sure it was your children." Careah began to quiver. "Glory be, 'your children' could mean every child."

La'no called Eli, "I know it's early morning, but this is an emergency get the T.V. station to broadcast this message: have everyone check on their kids. I mean now, pronto!"

It wasn't long before every family having small children from newborn to one year old found that their children were missing from their beds.

Ke'oney got drunk, tripped and fell out of heaven, landed in a pool of water on earth. She got to dry ground. There was a Kakel bird kakeling; she thought the bird was making fun of her. She got angry changed the bird into a rabbit that laid colored eggs. Since then, they call it Ke'oney day.

It is soon Ke'oney day; they need little kids for sacrifice on their-altars, to honor their goddess of pleasure, Ke'oney.

Rush added, "We will get one of those Morons, and offer him a contract he can't refuse."

King Flash said, "We'll take my Courser, Mitch; it's faster and quieter, and flies high above the clouds. They can't see us but we can see them."

They took off and were there in minutes.

Rush said, "We are in luck; I see one of the jerks with his back to us."

King Flash glided down landed behind the 15-foot Moron. Rush jumped out of the ship, and before he knew what hit him, Rush and Lippy pulled him into the ship, then flew up 1,000 feet. The Moron was so scared, he froze with fright.

Flash asked the Moron in his language, "Where are the children you people kidnaped?" The Moron never saw an aquatic man before; all he could do was shake. "I'll get him to talk."

He and one of his men grabbed the Moron, took him, and opened the door, making like they were going to kick him out. He started talking six mile a minute.

Flash called La'no, "We have pinpointed the place where the children are."

La'no made it clear: "We go after the children first, then we go after the main army of Morons. We will get the children. That is a promise I made to their parents."

Although the Morons were 15-feet tall, they were no match for the people who love their children and most of all their God. They stormed the entrance of the cave, and every Moron guarding the Children got an address unknown. All 500 children were carried aboard spaceships, headed home to overjoyed parents.

La'no asked Lippy, "Do you know where the army of Morons are located?"

"I heard they are somewhere north of Moab. I know if they see or hear you, they will go underground."

Lano asked, "What I want to know is how they got close to 500 little kids without us knowing. We will take only air-cars that fly without much noise. Moab is a large territory. We will need every air car we can get. Lippy, how will we know them when we see them?"

"If I'm right, they all wear red sweatbands. When they do their thing, they all wear miters to honor their fish god, and their goddess of pleasure Ke'oney."

Lano ordered, "Every man and woman who can handle a bow, I mean everyone, no exception, go after the kidnappers!"

Careah had all the ladies ready who were with her in the war. They had more experience than the men. Kedar also had a few ladies who knew how to handle the bow. One of the ladies in Kedar's outfit said, "We are like the mother bear with cubs, don't mess with our kids either."

La'no ordered the Elite Army, Marines, and Navy to carry their Lazar pistols, and 900 angry men with their side arms called Stingrays to get every worshiper of the false goddess Ke'oney.

All air ships headed to the country above Moab close to Petra. Lippy spotted their camp. Flash gave the order to land in the middle of the camp. All air crafts landed quickly to prevent any of the Morons escaping. The ladies filled the air with arrows. Men using their Stingrays and the armed forces filled the air with Lazars shots, ending the battle in short time. The battle was more of a show than a good fight. All 1,000-plus Morons also got an address unknown.

La'no called a special Shepherds' meeting. Every Shepherd filled the hall early. La'no called for order; the room got very quiet. He opened with the statement everyone expected.

"At this moment, no one is above suspicion. Right now, whoever helped the Morons has to be jumpy, afraid, not to make any false moves, trying to act natural. Someone had to have helped those Morons; 500 or more didn't get in here without help. Does anyone of you have any ideas who it might be? I know you here are not guilty; you would be sweating. I'll be like hound dog, sniffing every place you never would believe. Nothing in this world will stop us from getting them.

"How can a person do this dastardly act? I'm going to be like a hound dog after a rabbit.

Now since we got the children, we will get every jack ~^*^~. I mean every one!"

La'no asked, "Does anyone know anything about how this happened? I'll follow any tips, think hard, think back, see or hear anything that may be strange to you at the time. Has anyone left Hi-Why-O? I don't care where they go; we will find them. We will use every means there is, we will not rest until you are in our hands. There will be no barging, every one of you will wish you were not born. We will show no mercy; you will get what you deserve. The trees will not hide you. The rocks will turn you away. When we find you, the people will tear you to sherds. You are doomed, you know it by now."

It was late evening when La'no got a call. We want to give ourselves up."

"Okay, Jays, come in, don't stop anywhere. The people will mob you, you can come in the back door."

They entered La'no's office. He said, "Sit down. I promise you will get a fair trial; the Shepherds will not judge you, the people who had children kidnaped will judge you. You can tell me why you did this horrible, horrible act."

The Jays said, "We took our twins outside to watch the volcano spew its flames in the air. Two strangers grabbed our twins and threatened to kill them if we told anyone they were there, we would get them back if we did what they said.

"After they left, we knew they saw the door gate. We are so sorry we didn't tell you, but they had our twins."

La'no looked them square in their eyes.

"Yes, you should have told me, I would have gotten your twins back before they got very far."

In the morning, they entered the judgement hall. People were crying, "Death, death, death."

La'no held his hand up for silence.

"I have thought about what they did; it made me mad, very mad, but since you all got your children back safely, think about the Di-No-drag-Compound. (*Dinosaur and Dragon Compound*) Giving them one or three years may serve them right.

"Remember what happens in three years. Take your time think about it before you may regret what you do first and be sorry. Think on it until tomorrow then give your verdict. Put yourself in their shoes."

The next morning, everyone who was involved was in the hall; it was buzzing like a bee hive when someone tries to get their honey. La'no asked for silence. It got so quiet, like in a morgue. Ken and his wife Liza were shaking like leaves on trees on a windy day.

La'no asked, "Have you reached a verdict?"

Tom Babs acting as their spokesmen replied, "Yes, we all agreed on the verdict."

La'no inquired, "What is your verdict?"

"We all agree, Ken and Liza spend one year in the Di-No-Drag Compound, suspended."

There was deadly silence, then a rapture of a standing ovation.

La'no had the final say, "So be it, with a condition, Ken and Liza, you must be beneficial to your country and help those in need, not financially but through manual help. Ken, you will keep your job; the company you work at needs your expertise. Most of all, you are needed being an engineer of physics. From this hour on, the door gates will be guarded by two men with Lazar pistols, 24 hours a day until we leave this world."

Mary the mother of Yeshua received a message via the school John was attending.

"It has come to our attention some evil vile men robbed and killed his parents. The school wants to know if you know someone will raise and take good care of him. His grades in Hebrew and Latin are the highest in his class."

Mary said, "If no one will take him, I will take him. We asked him if he knew when he was born, he said in the winter time. We do think he is about 16 years old, give or take a month or two. His parents were silver and gold smiths. That's why they were killed, for their gold and silver.

These Rouges killed other wealthy people in John's home town. Roman soldiers finally caught them and hung them on crosses."

Ugly buzzards wait in the background until those on crosses are dead, the first thing the buzzards go for is the eyes. What is left of the corpses are thrown into the burning garbage dump, also the crosses burned. It is recorded most of the corruptible lived in Nazareth; even the law stayed away from there. Yeshua lived there until He had to finish the Nazarites rites, then went on his way to the cross of Calvary.

La'no and his friends went with Yeshua to Peter's home, his mother-in-law was in bed with a fever. Yeshua touched her hand, and she got up made them all a meal. After He healed many, He said, "We are needed at Simon's home. His mother-in-law is sick."

He healed her, she got up and made them a meal.

People brought sick and demon possessed people for Yeshua to heal; all the sick were healed and demons rebuked.

The demons shouted, "Truly, You are the Son of God," then the demons looked at La'no and his friends and said, "We know you also, and you two with wings, pretending to be something you are not. Leave us alone, or we will make it miserable for you when you are not expecting it."

Yeshua rebuked them with a stern voice, "Go back where you came from."

Later toward sunset, La'no asked Yeshua, "Do you think people you heal will appreciate what you done for them?"

He replied, "I know most do; a few will forget what took place here. But I got to tell them about my Father."

La'no shook Yeshua's hand, "We will see you in a couple days. We love hearing you talk about your Father."

Yeshua hugged La'no, "I thank you all for your support my friends and that's for sure."

Yeshua was watching fishermen pull up empty nets. He put his hands to his mouth yelled, "Put your nets on the other side of your boat."

They yelled back, "Sir, we fished all night, no fish."

"Will you do as I say? Put your nets on the other side of your boat."

One of the fishermen said, "He is no fisherman. No hook marks on his body… He doesn't know an anchor from a fish hook. Let's go home, my wife needs me to get wood to cook fish which we don't have."

Another fisherman asked, "What do we got to lose? Let's do it. It will make Him happy."

Over the side, the nets went. Before the nets reached the bottom, they were overloaded with more than the nets could hold. They had to call for other boats to help, or they would sink. Four boats of fish ready for market! They went to thank the stranger.

La'no said, "Those fish only come up at night and close to shore, never out in the deep."

Peter, James, and Simon, the son of Zebedee, fell at Yeshua's feet, "Go away from us, Lord, we are sinful men."

Yeshua replied, "That's okay for now. If you follow me, I will make you fisher of men."

One of the fishermen asked, "What's fisher of men."

Yeshua told them what they had to do to be fisher of men. They gladly said, "Yes."

They took their fish to market, then went with Yeshua.

La'no and his friends shook Yeshua's hand saying, "We will see you later."

La'no was standing with Yeshua when a man with leprosy came to Yeshua on his knees begged him saying, "If you are willing, make me clean."

Yeshua replied, "Yes I'm willing." He touched him, and he was cleaned. "Now go and tell no one who healed you. Go and show the priest and offer the sacrifice Moses commanded."

La'no said, "I feel he will tell everyone he meets."

Yeshua added, "I'm positive he will. Many with one of the most horrible contagious, smelly, shocking, disease called leprosy were healed that day. All went to their loved ones, a new, clean, over-joyous person.

Yeshua and La'no were walking near the tax collector's booth. Yeshua said to La'no He had been talking to Matthew for several weeks about going with Him in His ministry.

"He would work several days, then with Me the other days," Yeshua said, "Matthew is going to be a great disciple, and later he will record our ministry, which would be a benefit for mankind."

La'no's watch-phone buzzed. "There's a huge fire out of control in a hotel in Hi-Why-G."

After telling Yeshua about the fire, La'no excused himself. Getting to the fire, he asked, "what happened?"

"There was a massive explosion. Our largest hotel on fire burned out of control blew several blocks in every direction. Fire spread to other buildings, then other buildings. Block after block burst into huge flames."

"Why aren't the fire trucks putting the fires out?"

"The main water system is sabotaged, water pump beyond repair, and all parts damaged and water poisoned. The hotel and four other buildings burned to the ground. More are starting to burn; there's nothing to stop them. Thick smoke filled their paradise. The fans started as soon as the fire started pushing the smoke out the active volcano."

La'no, King Flash, Eli, Rush, and Kedar watched helplessly. Their whole country soon would burn to the ground. Every fire company came from all over Hi-Why-O and started pumping water from the poisoned lakes. Poison filled the air. Soon they had to stop the pumping.

Several Shepherds suggested leaving for the outside.

Kedar said, "Hold it, just hold it, let's all put our heads together, and find a suitable solution to our problem before it's too late for ever one."

Those standing with their hands in their pockets yelled, "What do you have in mind?"

"Well," replied Kedar, "remember we fought the demon war with fire, so let's do it again."

La'no replied, "I'm beginning to see what Kedar means."

Several Shepherds complained, "You are all crazy!"

La'no shot back, "I may be crazy, but I'm not stupid. So, let's get every bottle we can find and make bottle bombs, get all of the rockets we can find. We blow all the buildings about a hundred yards around the burning buildings down to the ground. Then take all bulldozers, clean a path all the way around the fire, now. I mean now."

A lady Shepherd screamed, "You can't do that people live in those buildings!"

Rush snapped at her, "Lady, what in the hell do you want us to do then?"

La'no broke in, "We are not ready to leave here for our new world. We have to do what we have to do and now. So, we blow all the building needed to get ahead of the fire. All firemen are in charge of the job that has to be done. That way everything will be done right.

"They will have to work in shifts because it will take several days and nights to do it right. The ladies aids from all churches can keep food and drinks ready to serve the firefighters. Rush and Eli can take air tankers and get fresh pure drinking water from the outside.

"Now that things started to slow down, does anyone know how this disaster started?"

King Flash spoke up, "This fire was no accident. I smelled dry gas, and there is no dry gas close here. Every camera was burned to a crisp. I heard the last explosion; it was the building housing the dry gas."

Kedar asked, "What is dry gas, and what is it used for?"

"It is an additive mixed with gasoline for more power. There had to be more than one person to do this atrocity. After the ashes cool, my men and I will go through the ashes with a fine tooth comb."

After several days, Flash and his men went to work sifting the dry ashes.

"Putting dry-gas in glass jugs is kind of stupid, and one spark, even a friction spark, will set the gas off. They didn't know what hit them. They were disintegrated before stepping into Hades. They will burn all the way through eternity. We have no idea who they were, nor will we know why they did it."

It wasn't long the smell of dry gas, and the unmistakable smell of dead bodies filled their nostrils, and they saw two dead figures burned to near dust, even their teeth were bonded together.

"Whoever did this didn't know much about dry gas."

La'no announced, "Those who have no place to live, move in with friends or relatives. Others can move into hotels, school buildings. We will not be living here very long, less than three years, so we have to make the best of it."

"I hope nothing happens between now and then. I wonder why no one else was burned or killed in this fire."

"You were with Yeshua, and there was Bobby Gee, the best preacher in the world, telling everyone about Yeshua and the rewards we will get in heaven. He was good, I mean very good. We will be getting rewards I never read about. The park was packed; those who didn't bring seats had to stand or sit on the ground. Pastor Gee is the one who saved us from certain death."

Careah and Wonder spoke up, "As we were close to the hotel, our car began making a funny sound, Else was walking by, and we picked her up. She may have been blown to her death. How could someone be so demented to do something as atrocious as this? It goes to show you, you don't know a person by their looks."

Yeshua was invited to Matthew's home for dinner. La'no asked Matthew if he could come and bring a few friends.

Matthew replied, "Why not, bring your wives if you want. I have two dining rooms, one for men and the other for ladies. If you choose to bring your wives, make sure they wear veils over their faces while they are outside. The people here will kill married ladies without veils."

"That's okay, King Flash has to put on a full beard, and Ador's sister Cayo, although single, will wear one."

As they entered Matthew's home, he kissed everyone on their cheeks replied, "Welcome to my humble home!"

Yeshua went to Careah and hugged her, then Kedar. Careah whispered, "Glory," and got tears in her eyes.

Kedar asked, "What's the reason for tears?"

She started crying sobbing with a big smile on her face, and answered Kedar through tears, "Look at my wings."

Kedar asked, "Are mine the same?"

Both their wings were folded close to their bodies. No one could see their wings under their robes. Careah went to Yeshua and kissed His cheek as Mar'ee came through the door way smiling saying, "Isn't He the greatest?"

Mary said, "He is my son like no other."

Both tables were loaded with all kinds of delicious food: soups, nuts, and fruit. A bottle of excellent blue bell wine, a bottle of red rose of Sharon wine, and a bottle of Chardonnay white wine, and a roasted lamb, on both tables. La'no's friends brought all kind of melons, dish after dish of casseroles, cakes, and pies. The ladies made two meatloaves smothered in Careah's red spicy gravy, one for each table.

When all were seated Matthew picked up a glass of wine made a toast: "May our friendship be forever."

Cayo in the other room picked up a glass of red wine, saying, "For sure I know it will be so."

Matthew carved the lamb at his table, and his wife Debora carved the lamb at the ladies' table.

Yeshua had a roll call, "Matthew and Debora, my mother and Mar'ee, Peter and Eve, John, who is not married. Now, our new friends, Kedar and Careah, La'no and Wonder, King Flash and Adorable, Eli and Tara, Rush and Cayo, his wife to be. Now if I didn't miss anyone, let's eat."

A group of Pharisees, Sadducees, and Scribes came by to see how many sinners were eating with Matthew. They said to Matthew, "How can you stand having those people in there so sinful, even Satan don't want them?"

Matthew pointed to the tables of food replied, "You are invited to share our food, but since you do not eat with sinners, it is your choice."

One of the Scribes named Adji looked at the food said, "Maybe we can sin a little today."

The head Pharisee gave him a sour look and exploded, "We do not eat with sinners, specially those who have wine. Wine will never touch our lips."

La'no said to Matthew, "May I say something to these nice people? Since you all are educated, I do not want to hurt your feelings. Before you say what's on your mind, find a pool of water and take a bath before your skin turns the color of mud, then go and find some Samaritans, tell them how much you love them."

Peter, laughing, said, "I would not have thought of telling them that."

The other disciples roared laughing. The ladies in the other room were giggling.

Won said, "That's my husband."

Careah remarked, "I'm surprised my husband Kedar didn't say something funny or derogatory."

Mar'ee said, "I'm sure Yesuah would have put them in their place."

Mary said, "Yes, and He comes in contact with people like that almost every day."

Ador spoke up, "Back home, we would not put up with jerks like that."

Yeshua finally spoke, "The self-righteous need more than a physician."

Kedar butted in, "A phycologist would be more like it."

Tara came to the door way saying, "A self-righteous person needs a rude awaking."

Eli, being a reporter, said, "It's a free country, let them believe what they believe and what we believe is true, so let's eat."

After the dinner feast was over, the servants came to clean up. Before cleaning up, they sat down and had one of the best meals they ever had.

Yeshua said, "You will have to excuse me; I have to go to Jerusalem to see a lame man at the pool of Bethzatha."

La'no asked, "Can we take you in the Courser?"

"No, I have to do things my way."

"Then may we go ahead of you and stay in the background? We want to see what happens when you do what you do."

"Okay, but keep your distance no matter what happens."

"I promise," assured La'no.

They watched Yeshua walkup to a lame man. Yeshua asked the fellow his name.

He said, "My name is Hopeless, I've been like this for 38 years."

"Okay, Hopeless, do you want to walk?"

"Yes, but there is no one to help me to the pool when the water is stirring."

"Okay, get up, and take your mat with you."

The man got up and took his mat with him. The Jewish leaders saw the man carrying a mat.

They said, "It's forbidden to carry your mat on the Sabbath."

"I don't care if it is, now I can walk for the first time in 38 years."

The Jewish leaders saw Yeshua heal the lame man. They wanted an excuse to find fault against Yeshua and kill Him.

The next day Yeshua was at the temple and the man He healed was there. Yeshua asked him his name and how he felt. He joyfully replied, "My name is Hap, and I feel great; never better."

Yeshua said above a whisper, "I don't want to hurt your feelings, but you better stop doing what you are doing, it is a sin. If you don't, remember I warned you, something worse may happen to you."

The man turned and walked away. He saw the Jewish leaders and told them Yeshua healed him.

That was enough for them to go after Yeshua and kill Him. They cornered Yeshua, accused Him of working on the Sabbath.

Yeshua said, "My Father works on the Sabbath, so I work on the Sabbath."

That did it, out came knives.

*Zap, zap, zap!* La'no and his friends saw the knives on the ground but Yeshua was nowhere to be seen. It seemed He vanished into thin air. The falling Sabbath, the Pharisees secretly watched Yeshua, knowing would He heal on the Sabbath. Yeshua knew what they were thinking. He saw a man with a mangled hand. He said, "Stand up, I want everyone to hear and see what I'm going to do.

"Is it lawful to do good on the Sabbath or do evil, or save a life or destroy a life? Now stretch out your hand."

Instantly his hand was completely healed. The Pharisees were furious and planned to kill Him. Yeshua simply vanished.

La'no was looking over the prints; something wasn't right. He went over the prints again. His gut felt something was not right, his eyes could not see what it was. He had no choice but to call Ken Jay, who was still on probation. When La'no called the Jays, Ken and his wife Liza began to feel nervous, thinking maybe they had unknowing done something wrong again.

"Ken, I need your help desperately. Please will you come now, and I mean on the double?"

"Yes, yes, I'll be there as fast as my air-car will get me there." Ken grabbed his wife hugged and kissed her. "It's good news I'm needed by Rosh himself."

Ken was mumming all the way to La'no's office, wondering what La'no wanted him to do, not realizing it was a bigger task than he had ever thought. He was a little nervous entering La'no's office. La'no got up and shook his hand, saying, "Sit down, I have some bad news."

Ken began to shake in side of his stomach. He got tears in his eyes, thinking the worst.

La'no said, "I really need your help, more than you realize, Ken."

Ken began to melt inside, he felt like screaming, but asked, "What's wrong La'no?"

La'no replied, "I'm not sure, Ken, that's why I need your expertise. If you find the problem in these blue prints, the whole country will be indefinitely indebted to you."

Ken responded, "Where exactly do you think the problem is?"

"That's the problem I do not know, I know there is one but, I need you to find it."

"Are you sure there is a problem?"

"I believe so. Will you look these prints over and find it?"

"Okay, let me see the prints."

After a few minutes Ken blew air threw his teeth, saying, "La'no, you have more than one problem."

"I'm going to be stupid and ask, are you sure?"

"Yes, I'm sure as you're sitting there."

"What's the prognosis, Ken?"

Ken replied, "I recommend you have your best circuit board man to check them. Who is your electromagnetic specialist?"

"Mary Dee. She oversees everything that is done. I will double check, just to be sure. Ken, I want to ask you, is there a chance someone caused these problems?"

"Maybe, it sure looks like it."

"What do we do, and how do we repair what has to be done?"

"We need an electrical engineer besides myself. I don't know very much about atoms. My wife knows more about nucleus and electrons than anyone I know of. The problem is in the reactors, one wrong move, and we don't need to worry about going to another world. La'no, if you had not felt something was wrong, after we were on our way, we would be stranded in the middle of the Milky Way. Why are you not saying something?"

"Ken, we have to get the ones who caused our problems without letting them know we know! The question is why and who would do this, for what? There has to be a reason. The reason is the answer. Now what kind of trap can we set without them knowing? I can't call a Shepherd meeting; it may be one of them. I have to hand pick the ones to help with this."

He picked up his red phone, "You call or get your wife and get here PDQ. Flash, I need you here in my office. Bring General Rush, on the QT. Kedar, I need you here at the office on the QT. Eli, I need you here at the office on the QT. Admiral Lenz, I need you here at my office on the QT."

After telling everyone what happened, they searched for answers.

El asked, "Did you search for time bombs?"

La'no said, "Yes, no bombs, if there was one, and we missed it, we would be lost forever in the Milky Way."

Rush asked, "when will we be leaving this place?"

Ken replied, "I can't say for certain, there is no way to work on any space ships without tipping our hand."

Ken's wife Liza said, "This may work. We cannot work on any of the space ships without giving our selves away. I feel the persons who sabotaged the space ships, didn't do anything to their ships, right? So, we ask for a volunteer to get their space ship ready to start the voyage a year early, and we will meet them on the planet that is halfway to the one.

"They can set up camp for us to rest. Then we can work on our ships without suspicion."

La'no said, "That is one good idea. Are there any other ideas? Ken, you and your wife work at different jobs?"

"Yes, we both work daylight shifts at different companies, why?" asked Ken.

"I know two shrew brothers. I think they can help us to find what we need. I'll call my son; he will know where they are working. You all may go home and come back in the morning, remember this is QT."

Everyone was early. They walked into La'no's office saw two young men setting close to La'no's desk. La'no introduced the young men, "This is Jaydor, and this is Rayco, I told them about our problem, and both agreed to help us. They have been hired as janitors where Ken and Liza work. Both have security cameras hidden in their necklaces. Ken and Liza will help them to do their job as if they don't know much about the work. They have to know what to pick up and what not to pick up. Believe me, they are good at what they do. Each will give a signal when they know who is the corrupt person. Jaydor will signal with his left hand, touch his right side of his nose, then with his right hand, he will touch his left side of his nose. Rayco will do the same."

It took half hour into his job; Jaydor touched his left side of his nose with right hand, then with left hand touched his right side of his nose. Bingo. Then, without the workers knowing why, the plant was shut down; all went home. It took a little longer for Rayco to spot his dastardly person. He signaled the same as Jaydor. The plant was closed until further notice.

Jaydor and Rayco went to La'no's office. La'no had a big smile on his face, "You boys work fast. I assume you found our problem."

Jaydor said a man was causing one of the problems.

Rayco said, "A lady, I believe to be the wife of the man responsible for the other problem," was causing the other problems. "We think you don't have to look any further."

La'no said, "I'll call my friends to come in the morning. You two can tell us what you found."

Early morning, they watched Jaydor's camera. No one could see anything wrong.

Jaydor said, "You look but you don't see. Watch it again, this time watch his left hand, middle finger. See the tape on the nail of his finger? It is the same color of his skin. Now La'no, stop the video when his left hand appears. Notice what is under the tape. A thumb tack filed down, only a small point is barely seen."

Every one said, "Yeah, yeah, I see it now."

Jaydor said, "He uses it to scratch the magnetic tapes, which cannot be seen with the naked eye."

La'no said, "I told you people they were good."

Jaydor remarked, "Rayco should be here soon. His quest was a littler hard to spot."

Rayco called La'no's office, "I'll be there as soon as I get something to eat."

Jaydor said, "I should have told you, he gets very nervous if he doesn't eat."

La'no replied, "Come here, I'll have food brought in."

Rayco replied, "I'm in a restaurant and my order is in front of me. I'll be there as soon as I get this food where it belongs."

"Okay, we may as well eat lunch also. Please don't stop anywhere for dessert! Just kidding, Rayco, but get here soon as posable."

An hour later Rayco was in front of a group of anxious people, ready to hear what he had found.

He said, "It's all in the video. I was watching a lady who was acting kind of queer. She looked at me and smiled. I returned the smile, then moved to another lady to kick up unused parts. My intuition told me to look back at her hands. Boy did I get a shocker. Every person in this shop has to wear white rubber gloves. Now look at the video, watch her right hand, notice her ring finger, See her move the ring finger up and down the platinum strip. She has two rubber gloves on her right hand, and a plastic bag tied around her neck with a tube going down from it inside of her sleeve down between the two gloves to her hand where there is a small squeeze-able syringe in the palm of her hand, and another tube to the tip of her finger, a pinhole on the tip to let a micro drop of laundry detergent and lye comes, and she rubs it on the diodes as they go by on the assemble line. The diodes are useless."

Tara whispered, "I never thought a woman would do a thing like that."

La'no asked, "What is their names?"

"The Bens are husband and wife, Wade and Denise."

La'no called security, told them who to pick up, and instructed them to bring them to his office.

"We need six people to be judges. Tara, Flash, Rush, myself. We need two more. Bob is head of security, he will be here soon. I'll call Pastor Jim, he will make six."

Bob came in with the Bens in handcuffs.

They inquired, "Why are we in handcuffs and brought in as criminals?"

"As soon as Pastor Jim gets, here you will know."

An hour went by, the Bens were quite nervous. Finally, Pastor Jim came in and apologized; he had a death to attend to. La'no turned the T.V. on; it didn't take long. The Bens began to weep uncontrollably.

La'no said, "You know what your sentences will be."

"No they screamed, not the Compound!"

"Yes," replied La'no, "you will be taken from here to the Compound. There you will live for the rest of your livea."

The Shepherds asked, "Why did you do what you did?"

Sobbing, they cried, "We didn't want anyone to leave this paradise. We really don't believe there will be an earthquake."

La'no looked them eye to eye said, "If an earthquake doesn't happen within three years, and you are alive, you will be free to leave the Compound." The other Shepherds agreed to the sentences also.

Yeshua and his friends: his mother Mary, Mar'ee, King Flash, Adorable, Cayo, Rush, La'no, Wonder, Tara, Eli, Careah, and Kedar were strolling close to a small village near the Sea of Galilee. All were commenting on the forest of exotic trees, bushes, flowers, admiring the tapestry of the fields, beautiful trails, and the lake. It was so peaceful; no one was worrying about time or who was where.

Tara stopped Careah, "Since you two came here, more people have a greater sense of humor. Both of you have a happy capacity for meeting people with ease and possess a charismatic sense of humor. Kedar has more of a wicked funny sense of humor, which we all like. Don't change, Kedar, we all love you."

"Yes, and it's not funny; we all could be in the hear-after, had it not been for you two. It was washed clean by the flames of your love."

Kedar blushed, "No, we were not the only ones. You saved your world from an impending doom."

La'no broke in, "We owe you two a lot, even our lives."

Careah answered, "Glory to Glory, La'no, we followed the Lord's direction, didn't we Yeshua? Anyone following the Father will never go wrong."

"But still we owe you. Without a doubt, you have established an everlasting bond with everyone, and I mean everyone!"

Tara sounded off, "Something just hit me. A little Birdie told me there was going to be a party. What's this about a party, La'no?"

As La'no was about to explain about the party for Careah and Kedar, he asked Yeshua if He would come. "You are invited," he said

"I would be glad to come," Yeshua replied. He then had to excuse Himself; a little girl not far from there needed His help. "I'll see you all later."

Everyone said goodbye and good luck. He vanished into the air!

Seeing Yeshua disappear, Careah whispered, "Glory be."

A movement caught Kedar's peripheral vision. As he turned to his left, he thought he saw a dwarf dash from view. Without telling any of his friends, dashed off to the spot where it disappeared, seeing small shoe prints in the ground, he followed the prints into a thick under brush. Following for what he thought was several minutes, the prints were no longer visible, and he found himself lost.

Turning to backtrack, he hit his head on a low limb, knocking him backward to the ground and tumbling over steep bank. He hit his head on a boulder; lights out.

The lights came back on. Rubbing his head didn't help, so he closed his eyes tightly, squinting them shut, cringing to keep from yelling, frightening Careah and the others. Kedar tried getting up, even using his wings, but could not budge them.

"I must have bruised one of them," which one he didn't know.

Hurting all over, barely controlling his trembling hands, he felt silly falling and looked around to see if anyone was watching. There was no one in sight. At least that helped his vanity.

Never had he felt alone as he did at this moment. The place was empty of sound, not even a bird or a cricket chirped. Wrapped in the shadows of fog, his voice was muffled, and he couldn't think clearly because of the swirling in his head. There was a deep, almost primordial feeling to the fuzzy twilight; everything was twirling around, which he had no control. He wanted to yell as he faded into darkness again; he shook his head, to keep from fainting.

He hadn't walked in circles; he knew better, or at least he thought he did. Thick brush prevented seeing ahead very far. Getting close to the ground, he saw the tracks and followed them for a good ways. Suddenly, there were no tracks again… now what was he to do?

He moved in every direction, hoping to come across the tracks again. His mind flashed, "I hope I'm going in the right direction…"

He spit in the left palm of his hand and hit the spittle with his righthand forefinger sending the spittle south; that is the direction he took.

Listening for voices, or any noise, that may help him to find his way back to the others, he found there was no sound or movement anywhere; even the leaves were still. He wouldn't admit to himself he was lost. All pride left, and he began yelling, "Don't panic Mr. Wee!" hoping someone would hear him. He tried flying up, but the thicket prohibited it. Even climbing up through thick underbrush wasn't possible. Even though very little light came through, he continued on, limbs snapping back at him as he pushed through. He had just let a large branch fly, and as he turned, it hit him in the face and eyes. Rubbing his eyes, he staggered, tripped, and fell over a steep cleft. He did a couple somersaults before hitting something hard at the bottom.

In vain, he tried getting up, even using his wings. Looking up, the lights began to dim. Feeling a dull emptiness in his head, he wanted to scream, but fell into darkness, mumbling, "I hope I get out of here before it gets to dark."

When he had awakened that morning, he felt the day was going to be a special, wonderful, great day. He had good feelings before; a few times, it worked out well. Most of the time when it didn't, he would always say, "I should have stayed in bed." This was definitely one of the bad ones, maybe the worst. As he tried getting up again, pain raced to every bone in his body. Feeling a lump on his head, there was no evidence of bleeding. Hearing a bizarre sound, the hair on the back of his neck was warning him something was wrong. Almost afraid to look around to see what it was, he chanced a quick glance. Seeing tall grass moving in all directions as if something was frightened brought cold chills.

He thought his mind was playing tricks on him, seeing the head of a large boa constrictor. This really stood hair on end. The boa's head appeared again from behind a large stone. It hissed, tasting the air as it moved in his direction. Kedar's face froze with fright; his body stiffened, sweat poured out of every part of his body. What a penalty to pay for not letting the others know about the foot prints!

A rabbit jumped high in the air, breaking his horrifying stare, and he watched the boa slither after it. His body melted to mush and went limp. Would the boa come back for him? If crying would help, instead he started to pity himself, wishing he had left the shoe tracks alone. He felt numb, and very thirsty, but no water was to be had—and even if there was, how would he get it?

Looking around in anguish, he said out loud, "I wish the Lord would send someone to help me." The pain in his head worsened, and he yelled, "Yowl."

Cradling his head in his hands, he closed his eyes as if to pray.

"*Get up, me good man!*" It was a soft whisper. Then again, "*Get up me good man!*"

He thought it may be his imagination hearing things, and anyway, he couldn't move. Then a forceful command sounded in front of him. "*Well! Get up, me good man! I'd be not here all day to be standing here with me teeth in me mouth and a holden me patience to boot, whilst yoo make up yoor mind.*"

Kedar's head jerked up; his eyes raptured open. Standing before him was a small man, about half as tall as he was. He gave a sideways glance and eyed him with suspicion.

"Ah huh, I did see you a while ago, didn't I?"

"I, Willy Dunmore McBallyaskerry, had not the pleasure meeten yoo this very day. Yoo be looken mighty lonely campen there whilst I be tired of standen here I can tell yoo true." Stepping closer, he didn't offer to help Kedar up. "Make up yoor mind! Air yoo going to get up, or do yoo want to be alone a mite longer?"

Kedar frowned. Was he dreaming, or was this his imagination? Yet he heard and saw what was in front of him. Kedar, with a blank look on his face, wondered, *Did the Lord send this fellow to help me? Nah! Well maybe…?*

The little fellow's eyes looking him over were bright blue, heavy eye brows, a pug nose on the red side, uncut rumpled red hair. His ears wiggled as he talked. Kedar never saw clothing as this fellow had on, a red plaid coat with a hickey in a button hole. A blue plaid vest, green plaid knee-pants, revealing his argyle pattern socks. Shoes made of course untanned leather with decorative large square brass buckles. A bright orange hat in his left hand, a feather of many colors stuck in the brim and a cane in the other hand.

Kedar asked, "What is your name?"

"Me name air Willy Dunmore Mcballyaskerry."

Kedar replied, "That is quite a long name." He added, "Tis but a good one."

Kedar noticed from the start, the little fellow's dialect was not like his. He was using a peculiar brogue, lengthening some words, shortened others. At least he could understand what he was saying. Kedar stared at the small fellow with his mouth open.

"Well!" barked the small man again, taking his cane and tapping the ground. "What air yoo waitin fer?"

Kedar gave him a blank look and, struggling, tried to get up, but couldn't.

The stranger said, "Whilst yoo be maken up your mind, what be yoor name, me lad?"

"Me name is… I mean my name is Kedar Wee."

A wild look crossed his face.

"Air yoo kin to the McWees up in Tobbercury?"

"No, I'm afraid not," answered Kedar.

"Now why would yoo be afraid? The McWees air a good Clan, that they air. Now I tell yoo true, the McMitch Clan, do not mess with. The McMitch Clan air the bad ones, that they air. They love to drink brag and fight, if there be no fighten they be maken one," informed the small man.

"Sounds like a wild bunch," responded Kedar.

The little fellow frowned saying "Aye, that they air."

"I have a question, why do you answer with a question?"

The small man looked Kedar in his eyes asked, "Why do yoo want to know?"

Kedar replied, "Ah, poppy cock, forget it."

Willy inquired, "What's ah, poppy cock?"

Kedar smiled and said, "Well it depends where you are from, it can mean, a soft subject, foolish talk or nonsense."

Willy asked, "Who'd want to do that?"

Kedar rubbed his chin, saying, "Forget it."

Willy looked at Kedar with one eye closed asked, "Forget what?"

Kedar replied, "Nothing."

Willy barked, "Tis a lot of hullabaloo flyen around."

Kedar asked, "Why are you carrying your hat?"

Proudly, he said "Tis not a hat, tis me derby, and a fine one at that."

Kedar pointed, "Why do you have that thingamajig in your button hole?"

"Tis not a thingamajig, `tis a sham-rock for good luck. Here, me good man, I be given it to yoo, as I can see yoo be needen it more than I be needen it."

Kedar politely said, "I thank you very much." Then, with a worried look on his face, he said, "I see you're not lame. Why do you carry that cane, or do you hit someone you dislike with it?"

"Tis not a cane, tis me shillalah, and I be using it for walken, tis with me to day's end.

Be gully, I speck yoo be needen me help? I be not a hired helper, but when I come to one in distress, I give assistance." With a soft laugh, Willy extended his arm holding the shillalah out. "Now if yoo have a mind to grab hold of it, and I be helpen yoo up. Twill be beneficial for me as for yoorself."

As Kedar touched the shillalah, it felt like an invisible man had helped him up. His mind cleared from hitting his head in the fall, and overjoyed, he said, "Whatever was wrong with me, you fixed it, thank you, sir."

The little fellow cocked his head, warbled, "Fixed, yoo say?"

Kedar, laughing, said, "Yes, on my honor, I'm okay."

"Tis new ones, fixed, on yoor honor, never heard them words before," he responded, chuckling softly, "Fixed on yoor honor, yoo say, tis new ones." He chuckled some more.

Kedar asked, "What is your name, I didn't get it the first time?"

The small fellow perked up proud like, "I be Willy Dunmore McBallyaskerry, at your service. Me friends call me Willy D.; since yoo be fer-getten me name, yoo can call me Willy."

Kedar asked, "How did you happen to come by here? What part of HI-Why-O are you from? Are you a dwarf?"

Oh, oh, Kedar should not have called Willy a dwarf! Shuddering, Willy jumped up about a foot shaking his shillalah under Kedar's nose, ranted rather loudly, "In a piggie's eye, I be no misfit of a dwarf." Stuttering he said, "First, I- I, b-b, be a Leprechaun would yoo say from Ireland. Dublin I was to go."

Kedar said, "Really? Where's Ireland?"

Willy, looked at Kedar as if he was out of his mind, "Ireland tis not lost, tis where it always was, no one moved it."

Kedar giggled said, "Ah, that's good, I'm glad it's not lost."

"Are everyone Leprechauns where you come from?"

"No, Tis no secret, men air Leprechauns, ladies air Fairychauns."

As he was about to ask another question, Willy began strumming on the top his derby held in his left hand and staring at Kedar with a scowl on his face.

Kedar asked, "Why are you doing that?"

"Doing what," he asked.

"The devil's tattoo," informed Kedar.

Willy inquired, "What's the devil's tattoo?"

"It's what you're doing now, strumming with your fingers on your derby, that's called the devil's tattoo," instructed Kedar.

"The devil, yoo say, tis a new one too?" remarked Willy.

Kedar rolled his eyes and said, "Yes, and why do you do it?"

Willy chided, "Why do yoo want to know?"

Kedar responded, "This probably will be a silly question also. Do you always talk rough?"

One eye closed, Willy shook his finger under Kedar's nose, "Here now laddy, don't let yoor self be alarmed on this fine day. Tis a testy ol' coot that I be, I bet a rap, sometimes I be needen a good talk with me friend, else I'd be a wee bit peevish and later be feelen low for acting like a bloomen idiot. Twould you be excusin me for a mite? Me friend be setten me straight, before yoo'd say tiddly winks."

"Good," replied Kedar, then questioned Willy, "What's a rap?"

Willy snapped, "Every poor fellow knows a rap tis a half penny me lad."

"How in Jacob's Ladder did you get in here without the Belcantos knowing?"

Willy bellowed, "Tis a free country, taint it?"

Kedar pointed his finger at Willy, "There you go again, answering with a question."

Willy looked at him with one eye closed, "Yoo, never argue with yoor elders, tis not proper upbringing, me lad." Turning his back as if to talk to his invisible friend saying, but loud enough for Kedar to hear. "Now yoo be watchen it, Willy Dunmore McBallyaskerry, yoo know yoo be in a strange country, not knowen the good people here and the law, yoo must be careful, yoo could end up in the Hoose-gow. Yoo be not in Ireland, yoo lunk-head. Tis a good thing if I have a mind to mind me own business."

Kedar puckered his lips, "Hoose Gow! What's Hoose gow?"

"Tis a pokie," he replied.

"What's a pokie," Kedar asked again.

"Tis a jail."

Kedar replied, "Like a prison."

"Aye, now yoo be learning a bit this day," grinned Willy. "Now what yoo be wishen fir?"

Kedar shook his head no, "Gee, I never made a wish."

Willy snapped, "Aye, that yoo did me lad."

Kedar thought about it before answering, "The only thing I can think of, I wanted to get up and wished for a drink, I'm thirsty."

Willy took his shillalah and touched his derby and zip a bottle of Irish whisky was in his hand.

Kedar gasped, "No! No!" He tried to give the bottle back. "My wife will surely split my skull."

"What," gasped Willy stuttering, "Ur...ur. wif. Wife twill split yoor skull? That twill kill yoo? Ah, tis a pity, your wife yoo fear tis it!" He roared with a hearty laugh, "Now what kind of a wife tis that, twill kill her own husband?" Turning serious again, Willy ranted, "What tis the country comen to, a man afraid of his own wife."

Closing one eye, he squinted at him, "Or has she more husbands that she can afford to get rid of one?"

Kedar, picked up what he thought was an offending tone in his voice.

Quickly, he answered, "No, I'm the only one she has."

Willy wasn't paying too much attention to what Kedar was saying, said, "I be going with you that I should protect yoo. No wife ought to kill her husband, if she has only one husband. Now if yoo permit me to accompany yoo, I, Willy Dunmore McBallyaskerry, will go with yoo, I be protecten yoo. Aye, sir; tis for sure be golly."

Kedar informed him he could go with him to see his wife, but he would not have to protect him from her.

Willy asked, "Would it be now a wee bit of malarkey yoo'd be a tryen to feed me?"

"No on the contrary I am a little mixed up as to how all of this got started," remarked Kedar.

Willy with one eye closed said as if to talk to someone behind him, "Let me talk to me friend, he can help us to do what is good."

Kedar looked puzzled saying, "I don't see any one else here."

Willy turned to Kedar saying, "Don't be interrupting me when I be talken to me friend."

Again, with one eye closed, he pumped his thumb at Kedar, saying as if to his invisible friend, "Now then Mister Willy Dunmore McBallyaskerry, are yoo going to help this poor husband, whose wife tis going to kill him?"

"No! No! Please. I didn't mean she really would kill me. I just meant she wouldn't want me to have this bottle of whisky."

"Don't be interrupten me, I be asken yoo again. When me friend is talken to me and I be talken to him, tis not gentlemanly like to be dew-en…

"Now where twas I when yoo interrupted me and me good friend? Oh! What to do about this lad, whose wife tis going to … O … h! I now understand what yoo'd be tryen to say. You now say your wife won't be killen yoo. Phew, tis a relief for yoo and for me I hope to tell yoo. What tis the problem?"

Kedar pointing to the hill said, "I fell down that hill."

Willy frowned. "Someone who does something stupid gets a wee bit of praises from only himself. Now what in the whole wide world twas yoo doing that fer? Twas yoo tryen to come down that hill without yoor wife's help? Now if yoo knew she wouldn't be liken it, why if yoo please?"

Kedar thought to himself, *This fellow never shuts up*, and said, "Please hear me out. I was alone when I tripped and banged my head."

"Yoo banged yoor head, now that calls for a drink of good Irish whisky," expressed Willy.

"No, I don't drink whisky, it's too strong, burns my throat," he lied. He never had whisky in his life.

"Oh, yoo say no Irish whisky, okay, how about good smooth Otool's Irish Cream?" he interjected with a question in a friendly tone. "Tis the best elixir I can get me hands on."

Kedar thought, *I've heard elixir prolongs life*, and since he was being overly nice, he would take the Irish Cream. "Yes, I would like the Irish Cream," not knowing what Irish Cream was. He had good cream before, so there couldn't be that much difference.

Swish, the two bottles were exchanged.

Getting the Irish Cream, Kedar elated, "Fantastic."

"Tis done, now I be on me way to Canterberry," beamed Willy.

"Thank you, Willy, this Irish Cream will be fine with me, but please don't go, stay for a while," he said, trying to stall for time in case the others would show up to see this little Leprechaun.

"Okay, I be asken yoo, air we going to have some of Otool's Irish Cream or air yoo be keepen it to yoorself?"

Kedar replied, "Sure I'd like to have one drink with you before we part." He was trying to be friendly.

Willy barked, "What! One drink, only one drink will yeh? Yood be insultin me again! What am I going to do wich yoo?" His voice became rasping and holy like, "Saints preserve us! What kind of man twould yoo be, drink one drink, one good swig of good Otool's Irish Cream, tis a big insult tis be golly. Maybe yood be asken for a bottle of O'Leary's wine? One or the other, make up your mind, as I can move on before someone dies of thirst."

Before Kedar could ask or say anything else, Willy began singing an Irish lilt, while dancing the jig.

"Do you have to go? I thought you said you were going to Dublin."

"Aye, I do, but first I must go to Canterberry not to give a wish but to inspect the potato crop, to make sure tis Irish potatoes."

Kedar inquired, "Can you make any wishes come true?" He was only trying to stall him from leaving, until Careah could see him. "I can make a wish come around since yoo be asken. Should yoo spill salt, tis a good thing to do, throw a wee pinch of salt over yoor left shoulder by the hour of noon to keep you from feelen blue. Some say I can give a pot of gold if you can tell how old I be, but as I can see, I cannot, if yoo know what I twas meanen. But yoo can get a pot of gold at rainbow's end if it does not snow. I'd say to yoo, never wish on a star, tis too far."

Kedar politely said, "Thank you for the information."

Willy replied, "Information tis free, me lad, tis why I be sharen it with yoo."

Kedar flustered, "I asked can you give a wish?"

"Aye I can wish someone good luck if I receive a polite request," smiled Willy.

Kedar sparked, "Sounds a little wishy-washy. Do all Irish people have funny names?"

Willy snapped, "Funny yoo say? What kind of name would a fine upstanding Irishman be haven, but a good Irish one?"

Kedar very excitedly asked, "Are you really an Irishman, from another country?"

Willy's nose twitched, "Absolutely, what other person would be answering a nice young Irish lad like yourself, but a good Irishman?"

"Irish! I'm not Irish, I'm Bethish. I live in Bethlehem Israel."

Willy flabbergasted, "I twas under the notion everyone tis Irish." He began talking to himself, "I for one be asken me self, how in the world did I get into such a mess? Not Irish! Bethish you say, tis the luck of the Irish. Twas Dublin I twas to go. Somehow, I know not how I got here this very day. But since I be here to this fine country of yours, I be stretchen me legs a wee bit and twill have a look around before I go… what-cha-ma-call-it, Bethish, yoo say? Huh! Come to think of it, yoo don't look at all, Irish. No freckles, yoor dialect tis off on the Gaelic side. Them duds yoo have on, be not Irish linen which tis the best in the world.

"I see yoo put wings on… what fer? Yoo can't fly twas tried before. Yoo must be a bloomen idiot to be tryen it!" He closed one eye, and shaking his shillalah close to Kedar's nose, snapped, "Don't yoo know the law of gravity says, what goes up must come down, sometimes hard? Tis better to take them off before yoo kill yoor self."

Kedar backed up a few steps thinking Willy was going to hit him with the shillalah.

*Poof!* Willy was gone.

Kedar blinked and shook his head, Willy was not there. He looked all around; no Willy. Kedar thought he had been dreaming, but for the bottle of Otool's Irish Cream, he knew it wasn't a dream. He had taken a liking to Willy Dunmore McBallyaskerry. Feeling down in the dumps, looked around again hoping to see him standing close by, wishing Careah and the rest could have seen Willy.

Looking at the bottle of Otool's Irish Cream, he wondered what his wife was going to say.

"Well Willy said, it is good cream… Nothing wrong with good cream."

Kedar wanted Careah to meet Willy.

He turned to make his way up the steep hill. Looking to the top, he exclaimed, "No wonder I half killed myself falling down this cliff!"

Starting up, he froze, chills crawling up his back, heard a grunt of a wild animal before it attacks, dare he turn around.

"Where yoo be off to?" asked the familiar voice.

Kedar turned around yelled at the top of his lungs, "Willy D! Man, am I glad to see you! I thought you were gone for good. What made you come back?"

"Me memory tis going downhill a wee bit."

Looking around for carrageen (*nice soft Irish moss*) to sit on, asked, "Tis if yoo have a mind too, yoo'd be asken me to sit a wee spill and share that bottle? But no more than a few drinks, to put a sparkle in me eyes."

Kedar happily caroled, "Sit down beside me, my good man, and we shall have a few drinks and shoot the breeze."

As Willy sat down and felt a bit tiff.

"Here yoo go again. Now tis who yoo want to shoot? Someone who I don't know by the name of Breeze? Who tis he, yoo be wantin to shoot, and with what, yoo be not have anything to shoot with?"

As Kedar was about to poured the Irish Cream, Willy asked, "Now tell me if you have a mind to, why yoo be shooten Mister Breeze, that I be helpen to talk yoo out of? Or air yoo be rattlen me chain again?"

Kedar sighed, "Breeze is nobody, not a person. It is an expression, like, chew the rag, or chew the fat."

Willy snickered, "Holy shenanigans, never heard someone chewen the rag, chew fat gea, tis enough to be maken a body sick. What tis this world comen to?"

Kedar blusteringly replied, "No, no. What we do is talk and say what is on your mind, friendly like. Okay, do you understand?"

Willy spouted "Sounds like a good yarn yoo tryen to feed me." Willy took his derby off and placed it with the shillalah between he and Kedar. Wiping his forehead with a kerchief, he continued, "Before yoo ask me to remind yoo to ask me to give, no let me see what we be about to do before yoo so ruddily interrupted me."

Kedar shot back, "I didn't interrupt."

Before he could finish Willy broke in saying, "Sid not I, Willy Dunmore McBallyaskerry, ask yoo not argue with your elders? Maybe we should have a wee bit of that good Irish Cream first, twill help me memory, as yoors."

Kedar opened the bottle and smelled a little alcohol in it, quickly asked, "Will this Irish Cream intoxicate?"

"No, not if you should drink not so much of a bottle empty," assured Willy.

"Are you telling me the truth?" quizzed Kedar.

"Aye tis me truth," assured Willy.

Kedar asked, "What am I going to pour it in, or do you prefer to drink out of the bottle?"

Willy extended his empty hand, and *poof!* handed Kedar two beautiful crystal glasses. Where Willy got them, he didn't want to know. Willy motioned for Kedar to pour the Irish Cream.

Willy eyes glared, flashing sparks of fire, "Some people, not to say who, worry others with talken with their tongue before the brain said so." He twitched his nose with a wry grin flicking across his face. "Pour, lad, pour. What yoo be waiten fer? Maybe fer the saints to come marchen in?"

Kedar quickly poured each glass half full and was about to hand one to Willy. Willy looked at Kedar with one eye closed, "I see them as half empty, now bend yoor elbow a wee bit more, top then off with great care."

Kedar poured them to the brim and handed one to Willy.

Kedar said a toast, "Here's to you; have a good one, may your chickens lay lots of eggs."

Willy cringed, "You act like yoo be kissen the Blarney stone."

Kedar said, "How's that?"

"Now who be answering with a question?"

Kedar chided, "What's a Blarney stone?"

Willy came back, "I see you practice what you be preachen."

"Well what is it?" scowled Kedar.

"Tis a greenish black stone we like to kiss, called the Blarney stone. When kissen the Blarney Stone yoo get the gift of gab, and share a wee bit of blarney."

Kedar thought to himself, "This is a lot of boloney."

They touched glasses. Kedar didn't want to show he was a novice and gulped the drink in one gulp, saying, "Wheess, that's the best I ever had."

Willy growled, "Yep, thought so. Some people like to brag a wee bit. Irish Cream tis for sippen not gulpen."

He said, "I'll sip the next one."

Willy turned away from Kedar as if talking to his invisible friend, "This young whipper snapper, I gotta tell yoo, reminds me of a couple of good jokes to tell yeh. Mike and Patty went fishen… ah poot! How about this one! Paddy said to his wife- ah poot, Mike and the good Bishop… ah, poot!"

Kedar askcd, "Why are you saying, 'Ah, poot'?"

He said, "I was tellen me friend some jokes, and he heard them before."

Kedar asked Willy, "How far away is Ireland?"

He answered, "Tis not far the way I go."

Kedar inquired "What way is that, could I go that way?"

"Only the Leprechaun power can go that way."

A wry grin flicked across Kedar's face, an unusual funny feeling went through him compelling him to grab the derby and shillalah. He put the derby on before Willy could stop him. As he touched the derby with the shillalah, he was thinking of Ireland. In a blink of an eyelash, he was invisible. A whirlwind picked him up, sending him sailing through a time tunnel of different colored swirling light waves.

Hearing all kinds of hollow voices, laughing, screaming echoing, throughout an endless tunnel, he didn't have time to think what was going, on but he was scared—no frightened is a better word. He was filled with terror.

"Why did I take Willy's derby and shillalah, why?"

He was having a panic attack, and it was a good one. At the beginning, it was a sensational feeling, traveling through the time tunnel at the speed of light. He was having the time of his life. Now he was trembling like a feather in a hurricane and being dropped into a bond fire. Without any kind of warning, swish, swoop, a sharp hissing—his eyes began to close involuntary as he was cast into the never-never land.

Meanwhile Willy jumped up, a wry angry voice, shrieked, "Give back me derby and shillalah. Give back me derby I say, before all saints, who'd not be forgiven me for thinken what I be thinken. Give them back, before I be getting meself somewhat upset. All right, me man, you be getting me bull (*Irish temper*) going for me to lose it! Tis me duty to tell yeh, yoo be in big patches of bad trouble, yoo nincompoop!

"Tis so sad, I twill be signaled by Ban-shee (*female fairy*) that somebody, me, tis apt to die not of old age." Then thinking a horrible thought, he added, "I, Willy Dunmore McBallyaskerry, may never see me Ireland again."

Kedar eyes closed, hearing a faint hiss, before making a rough landing. His body rolled several times, and he slowly opened his eyes. He had landed on top of a high building, and looking around, what he saw fascinated him. It was a modern city like Hi-Why-E, only this city was on the outside. He didn't realize he was hurled 2,000 years into the future.

Walking to the edge of the roof, he took off flying around the city. Then he decided to fly closer to the streets. The first thing he saw set his heart beating wildly. He could hardly comprehend what he was looking at. A sign over a marble building in bright colors, *McWEE'S FLYING LESSONS*. Then to his amazement another building having a fancy sign over the door, *McMitch's Gym*. Hearing a squabble flew to the door sure enough there was a fist fight going on.

Yessirree bob, Willy Dunmore McBallyaskerry was telling the truth.

There it was, a large cream-colored building having many round towers with a huge neon signs on top of the roof high, reading, *OTOOL'S IRISH CREAM DISTILLERY*. Seeing other buildings down the street with unusual signs, he flew to them.

"Now I don't believe this!" He pinched himself to see if he was dreaming. No, he was awake. "This certainly seems like a coincidence, but there they are. *THE LEPRECHAUN THEATER and* the *LEPRECHAUN MUSEUM*."

Beside the museum was a large dark green stone, it looked almost black. With a wide smile flew down and kissed the *BLARNEY STONE*.

Across the street was the *LEPRECHAUN PUB*, and next to it was the famous *LEPRECHAUN HOTEL and RESTAURANT*. The next sign really made his day, the *Fairychaun's Beauty Salon*.

"Careah and the other ladies would be thrilled to come here. I wonder if this is the city Willy was talking about? What was the city he mentioned that was in need of a wish? Dunbe, no, Dub something, Dubling, no, come on think?" Then he saw the sign, "Welcome to *DUBLIN*."

"Oh!" Wow, his heart was over joyed. "I wish Careah could be here to see this beautiful city."

Hearing bells, he saw people entering a beautiful building, singing and praising the Lord. The ladies choir singing *Holy, Holy, Hallelujah King of Kings and Lord of Lords*. Someone shouted, "Praise the Lord!"

Kedar knew he was in the right city; these people worshiped the Lord.

He flew over the city again; the beauty was more than words could express.

"Oh by the stars! It's incredible! Just look at it! This is the most beautiful immaculate city I have ever seen. There are no other words to describe Dublin. If I were a writer, I'd write a whole volume on Dublin, Ireland, and call it the Emerald of the world. Why do I like this city so much?" Then remembering his dad said to him, "Your great grandfather came from Dublin, Ireland. Arriving in Israel, he joined a caravan heading to Bethlehem. This is where he met and married your great grandmother. He took the *Mc* off of his name and used plain Wee. Gee, I'm part Irish and part Bethish. Maybe more Irish then Bethish.

"Wait till I tell Careah she is married to an Irishman! I bet you that's where I got my red hair from. Willy said I had no freckles. Ah, when I was a kid, I was loaded with them and something else, why and how is it I can understand what Willy was saying?"

Suddenly a major burst of thunder interrupted his thoughts. Feeling a pang of sadness rip through him, reality was setting in. He had to get back to his Careah.

"What if I cannot get back? If I reverse what I did to get here, I should get back home." As he touched the derby with the shillalah, his thoughts were on Hi-Why-E and Willy. He was violently picked up, his body spinning, whirling through the time tunnel. Hearing voices crying, some moaning as if in pain. He was all alone whizzing though the twilight zone. What would be lurking ahead? Entering a blueish haze, he got cold, oh so cold—never had he felt so weird, but he began to get warm. A door opened revealing the entrance to Hades, a darkish red figure with a dozen arms and large hands bidding him to follow. Loud screams of agony rising out of the flames. Ghostly faces without bodies, their mouths moved in slow motion... unholy, burning red eyes of unhuman creatures emerging out of fire terrified him. Was this an ungodly nightmare? He felt unusually hot, blistering heat burning his flesh.

"Am I going into the abyss or the wrong way?"

The tunnel echoed his wild cries, "Stupid… stupid?"

His mind flooded with questions? "Will I end up in another country? Will I ever see Careah again? Will Willy want to crown me for doing what I did?"

He continued floating, spinning, getting dizzy, nearly losing consciousness, trying hard to

keep from passing out, then he heard a loud crunch, then a rapid thumping. Hitting something solid, stars appeared followed by a weird wailing, then darkness. Kedar landed hard, then bounced several times, sending fine dust flying everywhere.

A cloud of dust settled over Willy, a racking cough sent him to find cleaner air to get rid of the gritty taste out of his mouth.

Willy's eyes fizzed angry as a wild bull as he yelled, "Tis about time you be back!" He wanted to let lose his strident tongue but left well enough alone. "I be taken me derby and shillalah back. Tis time to leave." With a modified smile, he added, "The trip made yoo a wee bit sleepy, I shall be awaken yoo, so I can tell yoo goodbye and no hard feelings. Kedar, wake up, I say wake up! Wake up!"

"Wake up Kedar, please wake up," cried Careah. Awn took her kerchief and poured cool water on it and wiped Kedar's forehead and face. She smelled alcohol on Kedar but didn't make an issue of it. Taking a bottle of aromatic fragrant scent used to relieve faintness, she opened it and put it under Kedar's nose. Instantly he regained consciousness. La'no was the first to speak.

"You must have hit your head on that rock. You were out for quite some time. Next time you dart off, let one of us know. We spent hours hunting you."

Kedar looked around for Willy, no Willy. Holding his head, he wondered, "Could I have been dreaming about Willy Dunmore McBallyaskerry?"

Seeing the bottle of Irish Cream, he gulped. How was he going to explain the bottle of Otool's Irish Cream?

Tara pointed, "Look at that beautiful crystal glass, where did you get it, Kedar?"

The shamrock took La'no's attention.

"That thing, whatever it is, does not grow anywhere around here." Wanting an answer, he asked forcefully, "Where did you get it, Kedar?"

At that moment, Kedar needed Willy Dunmore McBallyaskerry more than ever at his side. The day quite simply had pounced a string of surprises on Kedar. Would they believe his outrageous story?

Several days later, Yeshua and His disciples were walking through a grain field; they were hungry, although it was the Sabbath. They each picked a hand full of grain and did eat. The Pharisees asked, "Why did they do this on the Sabbath?"

Yeshua replied, "Remember when David and his men went into the House of God and ate bread on the Sabbath."

The Pharisees were lost for words!

Then Yeshua said, "The Son of Man is Lord of the Sabbath!"

The Pharisees had no comment on that.

La'no called Kedar and Careah.

"I need to talk to you two soon as you can get here, or I can come to you?"

Kedar replied, "No, La'no, we will see you as soon as we get dressed and be on our way." Kedar said to his wife, "La'no sounded kind of upset, I hope there is nothing wrong."

Careah remarked, "We'll soon find out; he is standing on his porch. And he does look like there is something amiss."

As they got out of their air-car, La'no said, "Please come in the living room, Won is upset also."

"Careah, Kedar, where was Yeshua born?"

Careah replied, "In Bethlehem, you know that."

"No, no, what building was He born in? There is a rumor, He was born in a barn or a stable, you two were there... is that true?"

"For goodness sakes, La'no, and you and Wonder know Yeshua's Father would never let His Son be born in such a place. Who said He was born in a barn?"

"I think it was the Pharisees or Scribes," remarked La'no.

Careah said, "I don't remember when it was we talked with Yeshua about the Roman many times, I asked Him if the Romans worshiped His Father. He said no, the Romans honor their Sun god December 25."

Kedar butted in, "La'no, don't you remember the Prophets said, the Son of God would be born in the House of the Most High? (*Beth la jah*) And there would be no animals in the building where He would be born. First, let's start from the beginning, okay. Most of the know-it-alls don't know anything about where Christ would be born. All they know He was born in Bethlehem. And He was not born December 25; John the Baptist is Yeshua cousin, and John was born on a Passover April 8, 1 BC; six months later, Yeshua was born on the month of Tishri, October, our month. The day He was born was on Yomkippur. Now Tishri is harvest month. All farmers take their produce to Bethlehem to sell. They take wheat, barley, all grain products, figs, dates, olives, and olive oil, lots of wine. The ladies take their sewing goods; others take pottery to sell. People from all around come to buy or sell their goods. Bakers buy all kinds of grain to make their breads. Even the Roman soldiers buy their supplies.

"Now not just one inn, there were many inns. People took in relatives, others took in loggers. See how smart the Lord is? He made sure there would be no room for Joseph and Mary. The only place for them was the Lambing House, and it was clean and empty, the cleanest place in Bethlehem. When a female sheep is ready to deliver her little lamb, the Chief Shepherd brings her to the Lambing House to be born, so the baby lamb will not be hurt or bruised, if it is male, the priest sing songs and praises the Lord because it has no spots and is fit for sacrifice. So Yeshua had to be born in the Lambing house because He will be our sacrifice.

"Now, whoever said, 'Yeshua was born in a stinking barn, and born December 25,' is accusing the Holy Spirit of lying."

Careah took over saying, "Yeshua said you may call Him any foul name you want, but do not call the Holy Spirit any bad names or take away His Glory by giving the glory to another person or thing. If you do, there is no forgiveness. It is a sin unto death which there is no forgiveness.

"Now, La'no and Wonder, do you feel better knowing the truth?"

"Yes, we should have talked to Yeshua about this a long time ago," La'no replied. "It's like the old story, it's better to get it from the horse's mouth than the other end."

Won inquired, "Will you stay for dinner. Everything is on the stove and ready to be placed on the table. Careah can help me to get it on the table."

Kedar said, "That's okay with me; I could eat that horse La'no talked about."

La'no smiled, "Which end do you want to start on?"

Won said, "I wish Yeshua and Mar'ee could be here to share our food."

Her husband inquired, "Do you have enough food for all of us?"

Won replied, "Yes, I sure do."
La'no said to Kedar, "Let's get them and be back in a short time."
"How short?" inquired Won.
La'no replied, "How about 15 or 25, minutes max?"
His wife asked, "Do you know where they are?"
He jokily replied, "I think so or hope so. I'll call when we are ready to leave their place."

In his Courser, it took several minutes to get there. Yeshua was home, so was His mother, Mar'ee and John.

La'no said, "Come on, you all are invited to dinner." La'no called his wife, "All six of us are ready to take off."

Won said, "We go to the dining room."

She and Careah moved the dinnerware to the dining room in record time. After everyone was in the Courser, it took off and another five minutes, they were landing. Won said under her breath, "Thank the Lord we have plenty of food."

On entering, Mary had a casserole, and Mar'ee had a beautiful date and fig cake. Yeshua said the blessing, and it was a blessing to hear. For the first time, the four guests had creamy mashed potatoes with lamb gravy. After the meal was over and everything was cleaned up, they went to the garden to chit chat.

Yeshua said He had made his mind up. He was going to pick 12 men to teach and be His disciples. La'no asked their names. He said, "One is Peter, he has a lot to learn; Andrew, his brother, has a lot of spunk. Both are fishermen.

"John, who lives with us, is young and has a strong mind. James, my brother; Philip raised horses, spoke his mind. Nathanael is a farm boy; Matthew is a tax collector; Simon was a guerilla fighter, and Thaddaeus is an undertaker. Bartholomew was a slave loves to talk; Thomas is very out spoken, and Judas is a priest and will do his own thing. I love them all.

"Then my other brothers will follow me and give their life for the Kingdom of God."

He took His small band of disciples went up on small mountainside. He told them how they would be hated. They would be insulted and persecuted because of Him. He told them how they needed to pray when they would be in the tribulation.

"I did not come to abolish the laws but to fulfill them. I'm telling you now if you're righteousness is like the Pharisees, you will never enter the Kingdom of Heaven. They are a self- righteous, foolish people in a way they are to be pitied. I do not want any of you to teach a different Gospel other than what I teach. My Father will not like it. Now if you do, you will not hack it. I mean what I mean. Read my lips. You did not get the commandments just to look at, read, and study them. You will never regret it.

"Now, if a pretty girl walks by, and you lust after her, don't blame her for being nice looking; remember I created everything beautiful, that means you and your beautiful wives. I did not create you to be sloppy and not take good care of yourself. There an old story: A lady asked about using makeup, well if the barn needs painting, paint it. When someone does you wrong, it's hard not to take revenge, My Father said, He will take revenge. My Father and I hate divorce, but if one does not stop abusing, then the other should get a divorce. The innocent one has the right to remarry.

"Anger is very hard to keep under control. If you really love a person and that person does you wrong, try putting yourself in their place before you blow your top. Try it, you may like it. Hate has started too many wars, and to this day, not one of them has solved any problems. If a country refuses to be peaceful and starts a war in a peaceable country, it has the right to defend itself at any cost. I demand you protect your country; if you claim you are a conscientious objector, I will not defend you at you trial. Some wars cannot be avoided. The war in Heaven was a war started by Satan, it was one of the largest wars ever fought, He lost. Abraham fought the first war on earth, He won. Joshua fought Adonizedek in a war and won. David fought against the Jebusites and won. Sennacherib attacked Jerusalem and won. Nebuchadnezzar conquered Jerusalem. The Maccabeans fought Antiochus Epiphanes and won. Pompey conquered Jerusalem there was peace for 666-hundred years only with hatred.

"I, Yeshua, say there will be rumor and rumors of war. Titus will destroy Jerusalem. All of the Crusades wars will fail to bring peace. The Turks will fight and win Jerusalem and hold it for 400 years. Then there will be a World War that will prepare the land for the people of Israel. After that war there will be another World War, too; prepare the people for their land that will never be taken from them. Israeli Blitz will unite their country under the flag of David forever. Then the Antichrist will try to do away with Israel; He will fail and be killed. The beast and false prophet and his army will try to kill Me and My Army. They all will be cast into the lake of fire and brimstone.

"Then Satan will do his best to take over Israel and the world. He will fail and be cast into a lake of fire and brimstone; there He will burn forever and ever. Without a doubt, you will know I am the Lord who will rule forever. I will be the King of Kings and Lord of Lords. Until then, the world will go on as it is! Now I'm going to give you grades; five Bs. Sound good? I will Beckon you, I will Beg you, I will Bend you, I will Break you, or I will Bury you. Oh there is one more B, Burn you. Believe me, Be Born again, Before it's too late."

La'no went to see Yeshua for a favor; His mother Mary said He was going to Nain. He quickly ran to his Courser and landed near Nain in time to see several men bringing a bier out of the house. Yeshua asked her what her boy's name. She was weeping so loudly had a hard time saying Mark. Yeshua took the boy's hand and said, "Now, Mark, I want you to get up."

The boy sat up and hugged his mother. She grabbed Yeshua and sobbed uncontrollably, trying to thank Yeshua.

Yeshua saw another bier with young lady on it. Yeshua made his way through the crowd and touched her, and she got up and went to the crowd and mourners showing she was not sick anymore. The crowd stood, spellbound, mouths opened. Then pandemonium shouts were heard far away praising God.

Yeshua had a strange look on his face.

"What is it, Yeshua? We will get together soon, my good friend."

Several men standing nearby slowly walked up to Yeshua.

"We are John's disciples. He is in prison; he wants to know if you are the Messiah."

"You tell my cousin everything you saw me do, and he will know for sure that I am He. Tell John it will not be long he will be free. I'm telling you fellows that John did not come eating and drinking strong wine, and acting crazy.

"We know why he came, but the Pharisees, Scribes say he has a demon."

"Woe unto those who hate and persecute John. Nothing but fire and brimstone is their reward. They say I am a glutton and a drunkard and friend of tax collectors and sinners. Tell me who isn't a sinner; sinners are the ones I came for. I think there are tax collectors who do right; they collect what Rome wants and add a fair share for themselves. The unrighteous change more than what is fair."

People were bringing a small body on a bier out of a house. Yeshua walked up to the bier. To the mother with weeping tears flowing down her cheeks, He said, "I feel your sorrow." He took her by her hand and the boy's hand and said, "Awake, you are not dead just sleeping."

The boy sat up and asked, "Where am I?"

His mother really broke down crying tears of joy.

La'no stood in awe. Then he went to Yeshua, saying, "I need a great favor my wife is very sick. Will you come and heal her, please? Yeshua, will you?"

Yeshua said, "La'no you are one of my best and greatest friends. I could never refuse you anything. We do not have to go to her; she is not sick, she is okay."

"Thank you, Yeshua, oh, thank you so much." La'no had tears in his eyes. "Thank you, Yeshua, again, I humbly thank you from the bottom of my heart. I will never forget you, my Lord."

"La'no, you are getting a wonderful surprise."

It was several weeks before he saw Yeshua. While waiting for a call from Ken about their progress getting space ships built, he was recalling what Yeshua had told him about the surprise he was to get when the door opened and a tall stranger walked in and said, "Hi I'm your brother."

La'no stood up, sat down hard, and looked at the stranger saying, "You're crazy; I have no brother, never did."

The stranger said, "I'm Leo, I was one year old when I was kidnapped three days after you were born. Something kept saying in my head, get a DNA test. Finally, after a year, I had one done. I tell you, truly, I was surprised when I found I was your brother, I know who you are, the Rosh. I forget how many years passed when our mother and dad were killed in an accident. Of course, I didn't know they were my parents. I guess they never told you had a brother. I probably passed you on the street many times.

"I did see you when we were fighting the Ant War. I had a great group of men and ladies fighting until we ran out of things to fight with, then your son came by and gave us a lot of things to fight with. I didn't know he was your son either. Hey, I'm doing all of the talking. I would like to hear about you and your wife?"

"Yes, I didn't know I had a big brother either. Yeshua told me I was going to have surprise, and brother, you are one big surprise. I'm calling my wife. Wonder, I will be bringing a guest home for dinner. By the way are you married?"

"Yes, she is out in our air-car."

"Gauley jumping grass hoppers, another surprise! Bring her in, do you have any other surprises?"

"Not at this time."

Leo brought in his wife. La'no nearly jumped out of his chair.

"Are you Tara's sister?"

"Tara who? This is my wife May."

"Yeah, yeah, yeah." La'no called his wife, "Won, will you call Tara and Eli invite them to dinner also? I'll stop at the Ready Food Shop and pickup what you need."

"Okay, but no more surprises. You know I hate surprises! I'll call the shop and order what I need you pick it up."

La'no took the food into the kitchen. Then he took Leo and his wife into the dining room, and Won said, "Tara, where is Eli? I'm not Tara. Who in the dickens is this Tara?"

"Come on, Tara, no more of your tricks."

La'no broke in, "Really, Won, this is not Tara."

"Now you are kidding me too! I know Tara when I see her, and this is Tara. Tara, you are my best friend, don't do this to me."

Then Tara and Eli came in. Won's eyes began to flicker, and she fainted. La'no grabbed her before she fell. Tara looked at her and said, "Who are you what the hell are you doing?"

Leo broke in and said, "This is my wife May. You two must be twin sisters."

Tara snapped back, "Can't be, my sister was eaten by a wild animal when she was two years old."

Tara began to cry and hugged May sobbing, then May started to cry. Won went to both and put her arms around them, and she began to sob, tears flowing down her cheeks.

"Now I have two best friends."

La'no said rather angrily, "Those two people that kidnapped. You just said you were eaten by a wild animal and raised you as their own child. Are they still alive?"

May, still sobbing, said, "Yes, they are in a home for the insane."

Eli said, "You being kidnaped, what a story this is going to be! When did you two meet? How did you meet? Where did you meet? Do you have any children?"

May replied, "No, but one on the way."

Tara broke in saying, "Me too."

La'no asked his wife, "Do you still hate surprises?"

She replied, "Not this kind. But no more surprises of any kind."

He said, "Wonder, sit down, I have just a teeny-weeny surprise. This is my big brother Leo."

Won said with a smile, "The table is set and so is the food, let's eat." After a few seconds, she screamed, "YOUR WHAT?"

Yeshua and His disciples were at Peter' house to have a meal together. For an unknown reason, a large crowd entered Peter's home. An argument got started. They blamed Yeshua for starting it. His mother and brothers came to get him. The crowd said some derogatory things about Yeshua. His family said, "Don't pay any attention to him, he is crazy."

A smart jerk from Jerusalem said, "He is possessed by Beelzebub and casting out demons."

Yeshua replied, "How can Satan cast out Satan? You cannot enter a strong man's house unless you get the best of him and tie him up to get his riches." The crowd, some slobbering at their mouths, called Him every vile name they could utter. "Now I'm telling you can be forgiven of all the slander and sins you said against Me, but whosoever blasphemes against the Holy Spirit will never be forgiven. They sin unto death."

They brought a demon possessed man who was blind and mute; Yeshua healed him. He could see and talk. The people praised Him and said, "He is the son of David."

Yeshua gave one of the best parables He ever taught about a farmer sowing seeds. As he was sewing, some fell on the path. The birds ate it up. That is when a Christian tells a person about Christ, they hear but turn their back and not believe what they heard. Some of the seed fell on rocky ground; it sprung up, but had little ground and soon died. These people hear and say we will think about it, and let you know. They don't call; you call. They say we will go with you next Sunday, then they go one or two times then stop. Some seeds fell in among thorns as they grew, and the thorns choked the plants. These people believe and go to church, but soon they let the Devil influence them. Baseball, football is more thrilling. One Sunday won't hurt. Then next Sunday, a friend calls let's go fishing. The rest of the seed fell on good soil and harvested much grain; these people love going to church and have lots of fellowship with other Christians.

The neighbor farmer sows wheat; it sprouts and grows, but so does a wild wheat known as tear, and it is bitter and poison if eaten. It looks like wheat.

The tear will grow taller, and at harvest time, it is cut first and burned. Some people are Christians, other people look like Christians but are not. The death reaper knows them by their deeds, gathers them, and they will be burned.

The Kingdom of Heaven and the Kingdom God are two different places. The Kingdom of Heaven is now. We are living here on probation. We are to do God's will; some break probation. Those who do will meet the grim reaper. Those who do not break probation will go to the Kingdom of God, which is in Heaven. A man living in the Kingdom of Heaven saw a pearl like no other; he sold everything he had to buy it. We living in the Kingdom of Heaven are to do everything in our power to serve God to get that pearl which is Heaven.

It was a beautiful day; Yeshua and his disciples were crossing the Sea of Galilee, which is 20 kilometers wide and 30 kilometers long. It being a nice day, Yeshua went to the rear of the boat to rest and sleep. Like any large lake, the weather can change very quickly, and it did. The waves began to get higher than the boat. If this kind of storm continued, the boat would sink. The disciples feared the boat was going to sink and went to Yeshua got him awake. Surely the disciples didn't know Yeshua could stop the storm. They went to the right person. He rebuked the wind and told the waves to be calm.

Within a half-second, tons of water obeyed Him; the furious wind could not refuse His command. I believe if I were there, I would have been scared to death, not of the storm but at what He did. The other boats with them just didn't know why the storm became calm, but were glad it did.

La'no went to see Yeshua. He said, "I want to give you a body guard. There are too many attempts on your life, my friend."

"La'no, I know you mean well, but I must do things my way. They will end up at the judgement seat of My Father. La'no, I want to tell you something about judgment? Is that okay with you?"

"Yes very much so."

"Nine is finality of Judgement! Nine men from Adam to Noah, Flood. Nine—Noah was two days with his grandfather Methuselah, who died and buried, then Noah was in the Ark seven days to mourn his death before it began to rain. Judgment! Tower of Babel was nine stories, God confounded their language, Judgement.

"Nine plagues against nine false gods in Egypt, death of first born of humans and animals, Judgment! Solomon's temple was destroyed by Babylon on the ninth day of the ninth month, 586 AD! Saul made nine attempts on David's life; Saul was killed! Nine times Nineveh menschen in the book of Jonah, city was destroyed!

"Nine different baptisms, the last one is with fire! Nine covenants not to be broken! Nine of the Ten Commandments, in the N. T. Nine persons stoned, Blasphemer, Sabbath breakers, Achan, Adoram, Abimelech, Nabbath, Zechariah, Stephan, and a man named Paul will be. Nine afflicted with blindness, men at Lot's door, Syrian Army, King Zedeklah, Sampson, Eli, Ahijah, Elymes will be. I said 10 were healed; where are the nine?

"Last month, Jews tried to kill Me nine times. This month, it is nine times so far, nine days of confusion from Rapture to the start of Tribulation. Nine times men are told to love their wives and care for their family, 18 times, I said read my word, nine judgments on drought on grain, corn, wine, oil, rain, man, cattle, mountains, anything the ground brings forth, and anything done with your hands on the land. Nine widows, Tamar, Zerauh, A Woman of Tekoah, Haram' mother, Woman of Zarephath, Anna, Widow, Man of Jericho, Widow of Nain.

"Nine steps in the resurrection, Yeshua and Saints in Jerusalem, Christians before the tribulation, two witness, Tribulation saints, the 144000, Sea of Glass Saints, Tribulation Martyrs, O.T. Saints, last the unjust. Nine Scoffers, speaking of evil things they know nothing of, grumblers, mockers, false words, no fear of the Word. Believe others who think they know, false prophets and teachers, denying Christ, Vanity! Nine others: strife, boasting, ungodly lust, heresies, greed, carouse, self-righteousness, willing ignorance, envy. Nine other vain thoughts, being like Cain, error of Balaam, Korah's rebellion, ungodly deeds, false spirits, gaining admiration, believe not, sodomites and gomorrahs, ungodly deeds. There are nine ages; we are in the third age.

"Nine bad ones: revile, blaspheme, make others suffer, cursing, reject authority, deny Christ, flatters, mockers, complainers. There are phenomenal: ax head floated, mule talked, rod butted, water parted, Earth stood still, Earth backed up 10 steps. Earth turned upside down. Men walked in fire, a finger writing on stone, on a wall, and floor. 9x24=216 miracles in the Bible."

La'no returned to where his Courser was hidden took off. He wanted to get home, so he increased the Courser speed. La'no felt a slight pause in the engine and checked all gages. Without warning, the Courser nosed dived to the earth; everything was dead. He did glide it into a small depression of tall reeds. He quickly got the hatchet and cut small branches of trees, covering the Courser just in time. A band of rough looking men on camels with wild, vicious looking dogs stopped below where the Courser was hidden.

They made camp. Some of the men began looking for wood to make a fire. The steep bank prevented them from coming up to where he was. He was glad of that. They gathered wood and dried camel dung. They soon had a fire going and put a large piece of brownish meat, probably camel, on a well-used spit. They began drinking from a large jug. La'no could smell the liquid from where he was. It smelled like fermented fig juice mixed with wacko grass.

As it got dark, they began to prepare to go to sleep, with two guards walking around the camp. Even though it was dark, the full moon made it impossible for him to even try to go past the guards without being seen, but the dogs would get him before he got two steps. He thought he saw a spaceship overhead. There were no light to see in order to do what should be done. Nothing worked; even his wrist phone was dead. His Lazar pistol showed full charge. He should get sleep; he would need it, so he could work on his Courser. He thought of walking, but that would take several days, if he didn't meet any Bdelliums. Most were cut throats. He got back in the Courser and was asleep in seconds.

The next morning, he hoped they would pack up and leave. It was noon, and they were still there. Then he saw what he had hoped would not happen. Two of the dogs were coming up the steep hill. He got in his Courser in time as the dogs got at the door. The dogs began snarling. Then he remembered as a kid he made friends with mean watch dogs a farmer had. He split his lunch with the dogs and put water in his shoe; that did it, they became his friend.

The refrigerator door was opened from the crash. The lamb roast was on the hot Courser floor. It looked a little greenish. He cut chunks off and pushed the pieces of lamb out the bottom of the door. The water jug was cracked but enough water to fill two shoes. He opened the door far enough to put the shoes of water down on the ground. The dogs eagerly drank the water, wagging their tails. Now he had two good friends. Then one of the band whistled, and the dogs took off down the hill.

It was late afternoon, and still no sign of them packing up to leave. Then all bedlam broke loose. The two dogs he had made friends with were fighting the other dogs. Several men tried to stop the dog fight and were bitten on their arms. The men that were bitten killed the two dogs, left them lay. That must have prompted them to pack up and leave. La'no got two plastic bags and went down to get the dogs; he wanted to know what caused the dogs to go off the deep end. He saw foam at their mouths. He drug the dogs to hard dry ground, then took the dogs to his Courser. Then he went back down and made it look like animals drug them off. He made sure he left no tracks leading back to his Courser. He had a good feeling the Bdelliums would be back to check on the dogs. He was wright, but the men that were bitten were not with them. La'no counted the men, and there were four less. They saw where the bags were drug to and did a lot of talking then left. He lifted the hood of his Courser, what he saw made him hot—no, it made him hotter than hell. Someone was going to be in a lot of hot water when he got back home. He forgot he was hungry and thirsty.

It was getting dark, and nothing was in sight as far as he could see. He prepared to sleep in his Courser another night. He knew his people would be searching for him, and Wonder would be crying her eyes out, worried she would never see him again. The crickets and night creatures' melodies soon put him asleep.

Wonder was walking the floor, crying crocodile's tears flowing down her cheeks. May, Tara, Careah, and Adorable were trying their best to console her. Her two kids, Te'ro and Ke'no, had their arms around their mother, sobbing the worst they ever cried. They tried to contact Yeshua; no one knew where He was. King Flash and Leo, La'no's brother, were in Flash's spaceship, Bright Star, searching all of Israel up out of sight, they recorded everything they saw. One of the pictures showed a band of men and camels camped by a swampy area with several dogs. Kedar had Eli and Rush in his Blue Star, crisscrossing Israel also recording everything they saw; one of their pictures showed a man dragging two bags. Jaydor and his brother Rayco looked at all the pictures and took three of the pictures, saying they would start early in the morning to search for La'no's Courser.

At daylight, they flew low to the place where the men and camels were camped. They flew low and in circles. Jaydor spotted something hidden under cut tree branches; Rayco flew over the cut tree branches and turned the speaker on high, "La'no, are you down there? Come out with your hands up!"

La'no jumped out of the battered Courser, shook his finger at them, and began laughing. They called Wonder saying, "We found La'no safe and well, be home soon."

Wonder and everyone there began to shout and cry at the same time.

After they landed, La'no said, "Call Rush to get the Ekisties and get my Courser to the shop pronto. Someone will wish they were never born. Make sure those two bags get to the morgue and have the coroner do the best job he has ever done. I believe there are a couple of bodies a few miles up yonder. We'll get them also. Do you birds have anything to drink and eat?"

Jaydor replied "Yaw, sure what do you want to drink?"

"I don't care, all I want is something to drink and now before I die of thirst."

"How about a bottle of peach tonic and a hot Jim Dandy berg?"

"Now you are talking, when we get home, I'm going to see that you two are fired from your jobs. You two are now the new Police Department."

Jimco had the best sophisticated auto shop in the country; that's where the Courser went. The new Hi-Why-E Police Department took over the investigation of La'no's so called accidental crash. First they went to Jimco's auto shop to get all the facts of Jimco's findings.

Jimco said, "I would like La'no to be at the morgue. I'll talk to the medical examiner and get all of his findings. Rayco called Wonder here."

"Okay," replied Jaydor, "I'll call him."

Rayco said, "While you wait for La'no, I'll go ask Won if she prepared the roast."

Won said, "No, I had the deli do it. Why? Was there something wrong with it?"

"Just checking," answered Rayco. "Did you pick it up?"

"No, Te'ro picked it up? Now what's going on? Are you going to tell me, Rayco, or do I have to pull your teeth out?"

"Do you know where Te'ro is? I want to talk to her."

"She went shopping with a friend."

"Male or female. No, I'm not jealous." he said.

"Again, what's this about, are you going to tell me, or do I have to skin you alive?"

"Look Misses Be, I'm investigating your husband's accident, I have to ask you questions about the accident. If I don't, your husband will be the one skinning me alive."

"I know you do, my husband told me you and Jaydor are now the head of the Police Department. Tara came by, and they went dress shopping. Oh, by the way Te'ro would like you to meet at Joy's around 7."

"I'll call her. I may be late. I'm going to the veterinarian's over in Hi-WHY-G."

Won asked, "Are you coming for dinner tomorrow around 6?"

With a big smile he said, "I'll try my best. I really love your cooking."

As Rayco entered HI-WHY-G, he whispered, "This place looks so beautiful and peaceful, maybe I'll come here to live when Te'ro and I get married," then he remembered he had one of the worse battles here and fell in love with Te'ro. "That is the one good thing came out of the war, me getting one of most beautiful ladies God ever created."

Two blocks ahead was the veterinarian hospital.

Entering, he said, "Hi Gus, or do I call you Doc?"

Gus buzzed Rayco, "I have some interesting findings for you."

Rayco replied, "Good, good."

Gus continued, "This fellow is one smart cookie; he hunted rats, coons, and rattle snakes. He got the rabies virus from the rats' and coons' urine and blood, and just a drop of venom from the rattle snake. He didn't get any of the three items in here; he had to get them on the outside. We had rats before the war, but the Ants cleaned them out. I talked with the coroner from your neck of the woods, he, too, believes the arsenic came from outside some kind of fruit seeds or hearts of a green vegetable, maybe both."

Rayco bounced back, "It looks like we will never know who did this ungodly thing."

Gus reminded Rayco, "The only things you have is the lamb roast and La'no's Courser."

Rayco and La'no arrived at Jimco's auto shop at the same time. La'no started with his first question, "What did you find?"

"Hold on, La'no, you are lucky to be alive and here, I'm not kidding. First, after you took off, what prompted you to increase your speed?" asked Jimco.

"I don't know I just wanted to get home. Why?"

"Jimco said that's what saved your life. If you would have traveled normal speed, you would have crashed in the Salt Sea. Once you were in the water, the Courser door would have locked with you in it. There would be no power to open the doors. No one would know where you would be, and you would have run out of air in hours. I believe that's where you were supposed to be, not where you landed. The Lord was with you on that trip, La'no Bel.

"Whoever did this knew what he was doing. See this small box? It is still connected to the cooler; it shut the cooler down, and the engine heated up faster than normal, causing the Courser to crash."

"The only thing you have left is the lamb roast and this Courser to continue your investigation."

Rayco said, "I'll start with the lamb roast, and Jayco can start here on this dead duck."

Rayco called Te'ro, "Hi, it's me, one question. When you picked up the lamb roast, did you bring it right home?"

Te'ro answered back, "I went right home. I didn't stop anywhere. I thought I saw a funny looking car following, but it went right passed without stopping."

"Can you describe it?" inquired Rayco.

"Yes, it was blue or maybe it was light blue, or some kind of blue."

Rayco asked again, "Was it a small car, or a big car, a medium car?"

She replied, "I think it was kind of small for an air-car."

Rayco asked, "Do you know the make and model?"

She responded, "Maybe I should have stopped him and asked him his name and address. I don't know make and models of air-cars."

Rayco grinned said, "One more question, can you describe the air-car?"

"I can do better than that. It was like the ones we had in the war."

Just as he was to leave, Kedar landed in Jimco's parking lot. His display panel showed one of the jets had been replaced, it needed readjusted. Rayco walked over to his air-car and asked Kedar about his air-car.

"Most air-cars, when they leave the plant, are steel blue, your air-car is green."

Kedar said, "When La'no bought this air-car for me, the Plant manager ask me what color I would like it to be, and I replied green. So, they painted it green, and the one my wife got was gold."

Rayco asked, "Kedar, during the war, did you see a blue air-car other than steel blue?"

"I did not see one," Kedar remarked. "You were in the war. Didn't you see any?"

"My eyes were on girls, not cars. I did check with the plant manager. He said their records show no blue cars, other than steel blue."

"Did you ask Jimco if he painted any cars blue?"

"Thanks, Kedar. I nearly missed that one."

As Rayco entered Jimco's shop, he felt he was getting close to finding what he was looking for. He asked the sectary, "Did Jimco painted any cars blue?"

She asked back, "What color blue?"

Rayco smiling said, "I should have said any color blue other than blue steel."

She went to the computer pressed several keys. She looked at Rayco smiling, and said, "Yes, we painted nine different colors of blue."

She pushed print on her computer and handed Rayco the list of nine air-cars painted blue and the owners of the air-cars. He left, and outside, he turned around and went back where they were working on the Courser.

"Any luck yet?" The answer was no, and he looked at Jaydor and said, "I've a few leads. See you at the office."

Jaydor said under his breath, "I wish I had one good lead." Then he jumped off the Courser and went into the first machine shop he came to. He walked in and all he did was walk around. It was close to lunch time, and he went in to the office and asked if they were hiring. The lady at the desk said, "Not at this time. There may be an opening in a few months; one of our employs is thinking about retiring."

He said, "Okay, I'll check back then."

He went back into the shop. The men were in the lunch room. He marked each junk barrow, then he became a helper of the trash crew. He had marked A. B. C. D. on four containers, one for each barrow, then he took the containers to a warehouse to search for clues that would match the parts that caused La'no's Courser to crash. The men with him said, "We would like to help you, but we don't know what you are looking for."

"Neither do I, but I hope when I do, I will know what it is. It could be a small piece of small pipe, even small as a hypodermic needle or metal that doesn't belong to the shop. Since you want to become policemen, put on a pair of rubber gloves in hope there are finger prints. I think this guy is too smart to leave prints. If you see anything that doesn't belong to the shop's making, let me see it. Watch yourselves—don't get cut. It may be poisoned."

One of the fellows who helped load the containers found an empty tube of best steel glue, in container B.

Jaydor said, "Praise the Lord, you found a great piece of the puzzle!"

Then a fellow by the name of Wild Bil found a jeweler's gold cutter in container C.

"We'll find out if he used it on the Courser." Jaydor remarked. "Probably we will find something we are not looking for."

Wild Bil asked, "What would he use a jeweler's cutter for?"

"I don't know," answered Jaydor.

Sure enough they found a dentist mirror used to examine teeth in container A. After an hour or so, Bil's buddy Clem found a pair tweezers wrapped in oil cloth in container B. They still had a lot to go through. Jaydor found part of a human finger nail. Clem found a two-inch square piece of light metal; after weighing it, it was less than one half of an ounce.

It was getting late Jaydor said, "Let's call it a day, we can finish tomorrow."

Wild Bil and Clem said, "We would like to finish now, while we are here. We have to go to work early in the morning hauling trash."

"Okay, if you find anything, put it with the other findings. Before you start your job, come here first."

It was early Wild Bil and Clem were waiting for Jaydor. But both Jaydor and Rayco greeted them. Clem and Wild Bil were all smiles. Inside they showed what they found; two very small bottles of unknown substance.

"Okay, we will take everything we found to the lab. Can you be here early tomorrow morning?"

"Yes, we will be here," said Clem.

"The reason we wanted you here early we want you to take and use this master remote. It will open any garage door in the country. Just check double doors. Do it as fast as you can. If you see the blue air car get to the next pick up then call us."

Clem responded, "Some of our pickups are in alleys"

"If you see a garage door, regardless of size, check it."

"What if the door doesn't open?"

"If it will not open, right the address in your trip book, and we'll check it later."

"By the way, why do they call you Wild Bil?" asked Rayco.

"Well, I think it started when my dad was killed when I was eight years old. I became a target for all the bullies; some were twice my age. I would run and hide when I saw one coming in my direction, so one day I said to myself, 'I'm going to get even.' Since I was the fastest runner, I would throw mud on them or find old paint and toss on them on sidewalks. I'd scatter their garbage on their yard or porch, if I'd find a dead animal, I would open their door if they were not home and put in their house. I met a friend I might say good friend, his name is Clem…."

Clem was grinning from ear to ear.

"He said, 'Listen Bil, you keep doing what you are doing you are going to be sorry in the worst way,' and said, 'I'll think on it.' That is how I got the name Wild Bil.

"One night we got hold of a farm tractor hooked it to manure spreader and loaded it full of manure, I mean full. We took it to the main street in a large city. We put the spreader in gear and spread the city streets. I thought people would be raven mad, but most gathered the manure and used it in their gardens and yards. One day Harv, a black man, got hold of me and said, 'Bil, if you stop doing crazy things, I'll teach you to box. Think on it for awhile.'"

"Soon other kids started doing crazy things, and I got blamed for their dirty pranks. Harv bounced me again, 'You are going to do something bad, then you will go to prison. Like I said, if you stop doing crazy things, I'll teach you to box.' Everyone knew Harv was a Golden Glove Boxer. I became a fair boxer."

The next day, Clem said, "We found three doors that would not open."

Rayco said, "We'll take it from here. Give us the addresses, and we will let you know if we find it."

At the first address, they asked the owner, Obed, to open his rear garage door; they were searching for a yellow air-car with a red stripe on the hood. Obed opened the door; the first thing they saw made their hearts pump so fast, nearly giving away what they were hunting for. They thanked Obed and left. Rayco and Jaydor were shaking inside of their bodies so hard they barely could speak to each other. They headed for the next address as not to show any signs of give away, and incase Obed called to see if they were asked about the yellow air car with a red stripe.

They did the same with the third place. On the way to their office Rayco, asked Jaydor what they were going to do.

Jaydor replied, "You tell me, and we both know."

Back at their office, they called Wild Bil and Clem on what they had found.

"As soon as we get Mister Obed, you two are not trash collectors anymore. You report to the Police Academy for six-months of hard training."

The new recruits nearly passed out, hugged each other, and said, "How can we thank you? We didn't do that much."

"Just be ready. In the morning, we get Obed and whoever is in this with him. Now go home get plenty of rest and keep your mouth shut, be here early."

"How early?" asked Clem.

"Early," was the reply.

Before daylight, all four officers were at Obed's home. They knocked and rang the doorbell, no answer. Rayco used the remote to open the garage door. How should I say it, surprise no one is home? The spaceship was gone. Jaydor called La'no.

La'no said, "Keep checking, I'll be there as soon as I can."

Clem kept repeating, "I knew it, I knew it" over and over.

Rayco asked him, "What do you know?"

Clem replied, "Yesterday, I thought to myself, I should stay and watch all night if I had to. Maybe I could have stopped them."

"I guess they were onto us when we check their air-car."

Wild Bil had come from the neighbor next to the Obed's.

"I checked, and they said they heard the airship leave at midnight."

La'no buzzed in and said, "Let's see where they went."

Clem looked at his friend Bil and whispered, "How does La'no know where they went?"

Bil whispered back, "La'no knows every- thing."

La'no said, "First Obed was a Shepherd, and that gives me a good reason why he did what he did. All of their furniture is gone, all drapes are still here. All food supplies are gone. Jaydor, will you go and ask one of the neighbors to come here. I want to ask them a few questions."

As the neighbors came in, La'no said, "You are?"

They said, "We are the Herbs."

"Thanks for coming I would like to ask you a few questions if you don't mind. First, these two fellows are National Police, the other two are soon to be State Police. They can ask you any questions also. What are your first names?"

"My name is Al, and my wife's Jen."

"How many were there in this family? Al, you first."

Al said, "There was Obed and Miley, and two kids, a son and daughter."

Rayco asked, "How old were the kids?"

Jen replied, "Around 14 to 16, I think, and two adopted kids, a boy and a girl about the same age as their kids."

La'no asked, "Did either of you know they were planning this trip?"

Al replied, "No, but they sure were doing a lot of running in and out of their house. As you can see, their airship was in that big building connected to their house, so we never got to see what they were doing in the ship."

"That will be all," replied La'no, "if we have any other questions, we will call."

Rayco said, "If Obed traveled at the speed of sound, they are there where they wanted to be."

Jaydor said, "I'll bet my boots they are on a south sea island where it's good weather all year."

Rayco said, "They had to be traveling back and forth preparing their place to live."

Bil and Clem both spoke up at the same time, "We didn't realize at times there was more trash than normal; some of it looked like it was useable. All of it went into the live volcano."

La'no spoke up, "This is for you fellows only, no one else will ever know what I'm going to tell you. Do I have your word on what I going to tell you to keep it to yourself?"

Jaydor and Rayco said, "We know what you are going to tell us, La'no; we think we knew before you. We will tell Bil and Clem what happened, and nothing will never leave this room, a promise that will never be broken. Now Bil and Clem, what we are going to tell you may be strange, but we both feel you know what most of the crazy thing that happened is beyond anyone's imagination. Obed was a Shephard next in line for being Chief Shephard, you know La'no is our Chief Shephard, and I hope for many more years. Rayco and I know you know the rest of this stupid thing Obed tried to pull off."

Bil and Clem said, "We are so stupid. We don't know what happened; we thought Obed was getting a speeding ticket!"

La'no smiled and said, "You guys, thank you, and I love all four of you fellows."

La'no, Wonder, Careah, and Kedar were visiting Yeshua, His mother Mary, and Mar'ee.

Yeshua said, "Hey, would you like to take a boat ride?"

Everyone agreed to go for a boat ride with Yeshua. It was a beautiful day for sailing. After sailing for several hours, Yeshua crossed the lake to the town of Rakkath. When people saw Him come ashore, many with health problems rushed to Him to be healed.

Careah said, "You sure are popular where ever you go, Yeshua."

A beautiful tall lady not married with a hematoma problem tried to get close to Him just to touch Him, thinking that would cure her. Trying to get close to Him, she reached out to touch his robe, and she sort of tripped and grabbed the tassel on His robe. She felt her body being healed as she back away.

Yeshua turned and said, "Who grabbed and squeezed my tassel?"

One of His disciples who was there early said, "Yeshua, anyone could have touched you."

"I said who grabbed and squeezed my tassel. I felt power leaving Me."

The lady trembling fell at His feet, crying, "Have mercy, I had this problem and suffered for 12 years, and no doctors could heal me."

Yeshua smiled and said, "Because of your faith you are healed. You will suffer no more."

At that moment an official of the local synagogue by the name Jairus asked Yeshua to heal his daughter who was very sick. A member of Jairus's household came and said, "You are to late your daughter is dead."

Yeshua heard what was said and replied, "She is not dead; she is sleeping."

Everyone started laughing and make fun of Him.

Yeshua took Jairus by his hand said, "Come on, let's go to your home."

As they entered Jairu's home, everyone there was wailing, crying, and sobbing hysterically.

"Oh, Jairus we are so sorry for you."

Yeshua excused everyone but a couple of His disciples who were present, Jairus and his wife Sarah, then He said to La'no and his friends, "I would like you all to stay." Then He went to the little girl took her hand and said, "My *(talitha lambkin)* little lambkin, get up."

Immediately she got up and walked to her mother and dad. Oh what joy and excitement there was in Jairus's home!

La'no and his friends watched Yeshua take the five small barley loaves of bread and the two fish; looking toward heaven, he asked His Father to "bless this food." Then Yeshua had the disciples tear the bread into small pieces, putting them into hundreds of baskets, and the cutup fish in to hundred serving baskets. La'no and friends each had plenty of the food to eat.

Wonder said to her husband, "I sure would like this recipe for this bread and fish."

Careah replied, "Me too."

Kedar broke in, "Hey, there is a lot let over. Maybe we can get some to take home?"

Wonder surmised, "I wish King Flash and Adorable were here. They really love fish."

Kedar was in the back of the boat half asleep. By chance, he opened his eyes, the hair on the back of his neck stood out. Within seconds, he smiled and sat down. He had the ability to see further than other humans. Suddenly, the disciples stood petrified; they thought they saw a ghost walking on water toward them.

Yeshua cried out, "Hey, it's me. Do not be afraid."

Brave Peter yelled, "If that is you, Yeshua, can I walk on water to meet you?"

"Sure come on."

Smart Peter stepped on to the water and began to walk on the water. He said to himself very prideful, *Look at me I can walk on water!* That was it; down he started to go, yelling to Yeshua, "Help save me!"

Peter asked Yeshua, "Why couldn't I walk on water?"

Yeshua made it clear, "Without me, you can do nothing."

La'no called Kedar, "Hey, would you and your wife Careah like to go for a ride on the outside? I should stay and work on the space ships, but my wife and I need some time off, especially Wonder. Anyways I need to test fly my new Courser. The weather outside is perfect for flying."

"La'no, you know I have this fear of heights."

"Kedar, don't you know you can't kid a kidder."

Won broke in, "Kedar, let me talk to your wife."

"Okay, here she is."

"What's up Won?"

"Not much I just want to see if you would like to fly with us. We can chit chat while our husbands shoot the breeze."

Careah responded, "Okay, I'll pack us a lunch. Where are we going? Someplace in mind or just sight- seeing?"

"Maybe a little of both," remarked Won.

"Okay, we'll be there in a jiffy," Careah giggled.

La'no's new Courser was performing greater than he had expected. La'no had a slight smile on his face; they were flying twice the speed of sound, maybe a little more. Everyone was in plush seats, enjoying the view flying north up the Dead Sea. Jerusalem was in sight for only seconds, then Jericho. Flying up the valley of Jericho, the monitor showed a band of men beating a lone man, and as they were leaving, the man lying on the road was not moving.

As La'no was landing behind a small knoll, he saw a group of priests coming toward the man lying on the road. Instead of helping the man they crossed to the other side of the road letting the man lay. As everyone got out of the Courser, they saw another group of men dressed in gorgeous clothing, they also passed on the other side of the road. La'no asked the ladies to stay with the Courser; he and Kedar would go and see about the unconscious man.

Wonder said, "Hold it, there is a man and a woman on a cart stopping to see about the man."

La'no went to help if he could. The strangers looked up and saw La'no coming, not knowing if he was a robber or not. La'no said in Arabic, "I will help you."

The man nodded and smiled. They bandaged the wounded man, and La'no helped to get the man into the cart. La'no asked the man and woman who they were. They replied, smiling, "We are Samaritans. We will take this man to the nearest inn and pay for his keep until he has recovered."

La'no said he would like to help pay for his keep, and Kedar said, me too.

The Samaritan replied, "Please do not take this blessing from me."

La'no said, "Okay," and shook his hand. "Will you tell me your names?"

"Yes, my name is Jacob, and this is my wife Mary."

Kedar said, "It's a pity wives have to wear a veil over their face in public; I'll wager she is very beautiful."

Jacob replied, "She is one of God's most beautiful creations."

Without warning La'no's Courser was coming at them, horn blearing; it flew overhead, the horn still blearing. La'no saw why it flew overhead. Wonder saw the bandits coming back yelling to do their dirty work. Neither La'no or Kedar had their Lazar pistols. The Courser sent the Bandits flying in every direction, then it flew out of sight.

The Samaritans, smiling, said, "It was God."

La'no replied, "Maybe you're right."

He and Kedar walked back where they came from. They entered the Courser, Wonder's face was expressionless, and she kept repeating, "I didn't do it, I didn't do it!"

Careah laughed, trying to convince her, she did do it.

La'no was smiling from ear to ear, "Honey you saved our lives."

Careah whispered, "Thank the Lord she knew how to fly this new craft."

La'no said, "Okay, Won, move over I'll take us home."

On the way home Kedar asked out loud mostly for his benefit, "I wonder why that Samaritan was so generous toward a complete stranger."

His wife remarked, "You will have to ask him or the Lord."

It had been several weeks since they had been in touch with Yeshua. La'no was walking back and forth. His wife said, "You are going to wear the kitchen floor out. Why don't you call someone, and go see Yeshua."

"Hey, that's a good idea, thanks for your advice. Now who am I going to call?"

Won said, "I think King Flash or Rush would love to go and see Yeshua."

"I should go to work, but I miss that man. I'll tell you what I'll will do, I'll flip a coin: heads, I go to work; tails, I go to see Yeshua." He flipped the coin; tails, "I'm going to see my friend. I'll call Flash. He may want to go also."

As he pressed the button on his watch phone, Flash walked in the door and said, "Sure I would like to see my friend also."

Wonder said, "Someday I'm going to check that coin."

La'no winked at Flash and said, "Let's go."

They landed in their secret place and walked to Yeshua's home. His mother said He just left, He said something about the pool of Siloam.

Flash said, "I know where it is, it's about a mile across town."

As they got near the pool, Yeshua was taking dirt from the ground and spit on the ground making mud. Then as He put the mud on the blind man's eyes He whispered, "Rooakh," then told the blind man go and wash in the pool. A friend led him to the pool, and he washed his eyes, and in a flash, he could see.

Everywhere he went people asked, "Are you the one who was blind from birth?"

He replied happily, "Yes, I am the one. Yeshua made me see."

Others said, "No, you are not the one! It's someone else."

The Pharisees asked, "Did He make you see today the Sabbath? He has to be a fake; no one gets healed on the Sabbath."

"If you say so, but I know I once was blind, and now I can see."

"You are lying, where are your parents? They will tell us the truth."

"There are my parents, now ask them."

"What is their name?"

The man said, "Their name is Able."

The Pharisees went to the people and asked, "Are you the Ables?"

"Yes, what do you want?"

"Was your son blind from birth?"

"Yes."

"You people lie too."

"Well if you do not believe us, then ask our son. He is now of age, and is on his own."

The Pharisees found the young man in the City of David on the temple steps about to go in. They asked him again, "Are you the one this sinner healed your eyes?"

The young man said, "I do not want to insult you people, but a man cannot do what he did unless He is from God or He is God."

La'no and Flash said, "Three cheers for that young man," then went looking for Yeshua.

They found Yeshua talking to a group of people. Walking up close so they could hear what Yeshua was telling them, Yeshua said, "There was a rich man named Gibs. He lived in luxury, best clothing money could buy. He had more food than he could eat; the food that was left over, he gave to the dogs. At his gate, there was a beggar named Lazarus covered with sores, wishing Gibs would give him some scraps from his table. Poor Lazarus starved and died, He was not buried but tossed into the burning garbage dump. Angels carried his spirit and soul to where Abraham and other saints were. Low and behold, Gibs died and was buried with great pompous style and hired many mourners. But, he ended in Hades. Being in torment, he saw Lazarus with Abraham.

"'Please Father, Abraham let Lazarus just dip his finger in water and cool my tongue, for I am in great agony.'

"'Gibs, remember you lived in luxury, and Lazarus begged for your scraps from your table, but you gave it to the dogs? As you can see there is this great chasm between us.'

"'Will you send Lazarus to tell my five brothers of this place?'

"'Can't do that; they have the Prophets the Torah and the Cabala. They would not believe someone who came from the dead.'"

King Flash said, "I heard a fellow say he was going to sell his soul to the devil, dumb jerk; the Devil already owns his soul."

La'no said, "Yeah, I heard a stupid person say he wanted to go to Hell to be with his friends. If a person did go to Hell and be with friends, what a crowd to be with, murders, rapists, drunkards, and people who hate Christians with a passion."

Yeshua left the crowd and went with His friends, King Flash and La'no.

"You did hear what I said about Lazars and Gigs? That is a true story."

La'no and Flash, nodded yes.

Yeshua asked, "Do you know where Mt. Tabor is?"

"Yes, we both know where and how big it is," answered Flash. "Why do you ask, do you want us to take you there?"

"No, I would like you two and Kedar to be there tomorrow afternoon at the place where there is a small recess next to a double tree growing six feet from the recess. It is a place where you will not be seen. If you do go there, what you will see and hear, you must promise not to tell a person until you leave this planet."

They assured Yeshua, He would have their solemn promise not to say a word.

The next day at noon, they and Kedar were in the recess waiting for the unexpected. A crowd followed Yeshua, He had them stay at the bottom of the mountain and took Peter, James and John with him up close to the top of the mountain. Then Yeshua went a few yards and was transfigured, His face was shining brighter than the sun, His clothing was white as light. Suddenly, two men appeared and talked with Yeshua for quit a time. One was Elijah; the other was Moses.

Kedar whispered, "One could be Enoch. Moses has no muscles in his lips, that's why Aaron did most of the talking. This man talks like he has muscles in his lips."

A large bright cloud overshowed them, and a voice from heaven said, "This is My beloved Son, hear what He has to say."

Peter, James, and John fell on their faces and were very afraid. After the cloud and the two men from heaven left, Yeshua came to Peter, James, and John saying, "Tell no man what you saw and heard until I am raised from the dead."

Kedar said, "Why did Yeshua have us witness this?"
La'no said to Flash and Kedar, "I think I know why."
Flash said, "I do, too, there are several reasons."

1: Christ is the Son of man, in his sinless humanity will arise, in Glory, and taking with Him those who arise when he arise from the tomb. La'no said, "This will take place in Jerusalem."

2: Moses glorified, representing the redeemed who have entered the Kingdom via death, because of Yeshua placing His blood on the Mercy seat. La'no said, "That could be those who have died."

3: Elijah glorified, represents the redeemed who have entered the Kingdom of God by translation, of those who are alive waiting for His return, La'no said, "That is us, if we are the ones are alive."

4: Peter, James, and John unglorified, represent in the vision the Jewish believers will enter the Kingdom. Kedar said, "I believe they will get there after the Tribulation is over."
La'no replied, "You are right, Kedar."

5: The crowd in its need at the foot of the mountain portraying the nations to be brought into the Kingdom after the restoration of Israel, La'no said, "Including the O.T. Saints."
Kedar said, "Boy, when you're right, you're right!"

Work was being done on the spaceships; Ken the head engineer went to La'no.
"These ships have not been properly tested. We have to travel at least 5 Gs. At that speed, the ship will burn up. We have to get material that can deflect friction. The material we have will not stand the resistance. The material we have has to be mixed with, believe it or not, pig iron, the two mixed together will be perfect for the nose of the ships. We do not have any in here. Pig iron is on the outside, in the country far North where Red people live. I mean the far north above many large lakes."
La'no asked, "How much, and how do we get it?"

Ken replied, "We have 1,000 ships that need this on the nose of each. We need about a half-pound of pig iron for each ship, all together 500 pounds. Pig iron keeps other alloys from burning up and melting."

La'no gave his okay to take a space ship and equipment to get whatever he needed.

Ken said, "Have several men get 500 pounds of volcanic rock from the live volcano; we have the other alloys we need here. La'no, send someone else to get the pig iron. I need to be here to work on the jets."

"Who is the person best qualified for the job?"

"The brother of Obed, where he is I have no idea."

La'no asked, "What's his name? I can find him in a jiffy."

"If I remember the day I met him, it was on a Sunday at his church! Greg, Greg, that's his name, where he is… I think at the quarry, he is the foreman there. This guy knows more about rocks, stones, and anything in the ground. He is the one for the job.

"I'll draw a map so he knows where to go. One thing he has to watch for is wild bears, white, brown, black, and the ones that has interbred; they are the most vicious. They even kill their mates and cubs."

La'no said, "You tell Greg he has the authority to take what he needs, men and machines, including two Lazar guns."

Ken said, "Oh we need a good designer for the inside of the ships."

La'no responded, "I know the right person, Tara, my wife's friend. She and my wife are the ones to be trusted to do the best job. Tara is the best interior decorator in the country, not only it will be strong but very beautiful and comfortable."

Ken came back at La'no, "Do you realize it's going to take at least 1,000 or more people to get every one of the ships completed by the time we are to leave this planet?"

La'no responded to his question, "I know the right man for that job, he hasn't been doing much lately, He will be in charge of getting every factory working overtime. It will probably shock the day light out of him."

La'no pushed his watch phone on.

"Eli can you come to my office, say like now?" La'no looked at Ken, busted out laughing, "I know he can handle two jobs."

Ken replied, "Will you excuse me, I think I do not want to be here when you tell him of his promotion."

"Eli, I know you can handle two jobs, if you call Rush, offer him the job as your assistant."

"I hope he will, He and Cayo just got married; they eloped surprising everyone."

It had been a little over a week, and Ken called La'no.

"You will never guess who is standing beside me."

"Look fellow, I'm not a fortune teller nor a prophet, only my wife keeps me guessing, are you going to tell me or keep it a secret?"

"Greg is standing here and has all the Pig Iron we need."

"Great, get those heat deflectors done. Time is running out," replied La'no. La'no called the factory where the robots were made. "Kedar, will you tell me how far you are with the robots?"

"Sure, 2,025 of them is a big challenge. My wife and I are ready to program them within a week. Once we take off, the robots will take over the rest of the trip to our new home. We also have shuttles for each spaceship in case we need to get from one ship to another. There will be two robots in each Ship and three Robots in the hospital spaceship. Doctors, nurses, and their families will live in that ship. Once we get underway, we will be put in suspended animation most of the trip".

"Time is running out, all 1,000 spaceships have to be ready to take off when Yeshua is on the cross, and it gets dark for three hours. Every ship has to be off of this planet. I'll be the last one to leave. The Emerald Star is the largest ship because of more equipment. An x-ray that takes pictures of things underground and other important equipment, including my Courser."

La'no about jumped out of his chair and called Ken.

"Ken I need you back here on the double!"

As Ken entered La'no's office, he said, "I know what you want. A forcefield shield. A device such as an invisible plate or an antimagnetic screen to deflect enemy rockets, Lazar rays, or anything that may be shot at our spaceships."

La'no shot back at Ken, "When you're good, you are good, damn good. Do we have one of those deflectors?"

"The one we are working on works like a shower head spraying water, but it is to slow releasing its force shield."

King Flash heard what was discussed as he entered La'no's office. He said, "Why don't you try using a magneto to reverse the magnetic field, it will act like sonar pushing the switch faster than human eyes can see it work. Replace the old hand switch with a double magnet. It will detect anything 100 miles away and will touch the forcefield button and instantly the shield is in place."

Ken asked, "How do you know about magnetos?"

Flash shot back, "I do more than run a country!"

La'no said, "Now we can put one on every ship that will work perfect. Thank you, Flash, you saved us a lot of time. By the way, four days from now, we are going to the City of David to attend Passover and have Communion. It will be in the upper large room where Yeshua and His disciples will have their Passover meal. If you and Adorable would like to go with us, invite Rush and Cayo. I feel they will gladly come. I'll get reservations for 12. Park your Courser where I park."

"What time?" asked Flash.

"I'd say around seven."

It was Sunday, early morning, four days before Passover. Yeshua asked his disciples to go to town and get a young white jackass and bring it to Him.

"What if the owner objects when we take the jackass? Tell him I, Yeshua, need it for a couple hours. He will say, 'Okay, bring it back when you're done with it.'"

It was close the noon hour when Yeshua was on the young jackass entering Jerusalem. Behind him were 300,000 male lambs, all under the age of one year old to be sacrificed on Passover. Why people were placing Palm branches on the road before Yeshua, no one knows. The people came to watch and say there is the lamb that is going to be sacrificed for me. Since Yeshua is going to be sacrificed on Passover, He is the true Sacrifice once and for all. There will never be another sacrifice for sin. That's for sure and for certain.

La'no, Wonder, King Flash, Rush, Cayo, Kedar, Careah, Eli, Tara, Ken, and Liza were sitting at their table at the far end of the upper room. Judas was not present for this memorial event. Yeshua and the disciples were on the floor in a circle, each had pillows to lie on. Both companies finished their Passover meal.

Yeshua said, "Take the bread and break it, put one piece, and cover it with your napkin and eat the other which is symbolic of my body. The bread had to be without spot and baked with stripes and holes."

Yeshua said, "Take this challis and each pour yourself four glasses of wine."

Three cups were for the two door posts, and one for the upper door post, these, Yeshua drank but the fourth cup, he did not drink because it represented the shed blood of the lamb that He would soon shed.

Yeshua said, "This is symbolic of my blood, which is shed for you. Now take the hidden piece of bread, hold it up to show the world you belong to Me. You now may eat. Do this in remembrance of Me."

After the Memorial meal, Yeshua asked La'no to stay for a few moments. La'no told the others he would meet them at the Courser.

"Remember ladies, put your veils on when going outside," Careah remarked.

"How can we forget?"

Yeshua said to La'no, "Remember, communion is not a sacrament. Sacrament means to have an allegiance to, such as a country, or a person. Communion is a memorial feast, and you come freely."

Then He handed La'no a folded paper, saying, "I would appreciate if you do the memorial feast next year the way I have in this folder." La'no assured Him he would. "Please do the bread the way I did it. Then follow what I wrote in the folder. Will you give Kedar and King Flash a copy of the folder?"

"Yeshua, you know I'll do anything for you. Of course, I'll give Kedar and Flash a copy. Won will run copies in the printer. Yeshua, is there something wrong? You look a little down hearted?"

"I feel a little low today. That's mostly why I'm going to the Garden of Gethsemane. La'no, I'm asking you to do something I would not ask another person. I would like you, King Flash, and Kedar to be at the Mount of Olives. South of the large olive tree near the entrance of the Garden of Gethsemane. Do not bring your Lazar guns, and no matter what happens stay where you are. Once there, you will know why I'm asking you to do this. My help will come from heaven."

After getting home he called Kedar and Flash to be at his home 6:30 sharp. Then he got comfortable in his favorite chair, took the folder Yeshua had given him, began to read.

"Take the bread and ask the Lord to bless it. The bread is symbolic of my body. The bread has to have no spots but baked with stripes and holes. Take the bread and break it in half, take half and hide it under your napkin; it is hidden from view. Then eat the other piece. Then take the challis of red wine, ask the Lord to bless it. Then give the challis to the ones taking communion, each has to pour their own wine.

"First cup is symbolic of Gold, His Deity and Kingship. By His blood, He is our King forever. Second cup of wine symbolic of Frankincense, which is Christ priesthood. By His blood, we have intercessory prayer, giving us the right to go directly to the Throne of God with our prayers in Christ name. *(This can be the only time on this Earth we are sinless when we are before God at His Throne.)* Third cup of wine, He died on the cross, and He was embalmed with spices and myrrh then buried, this proved He was a true Prophet of God. A true Prophet was never buried without being embalmed. Our bodies will never be destroyed.

"After the fourth cup of wine is taken, the hidden piece of bread is shown to the world, then eaten. We will be united with Christ and shown to the world. Just as Christ was shown to the world after the resurrection, so we will be with Him forever."

King Flash and Kedar entered La'no's office nearly unnoticed, La'no was deep in thought. Had it not been for Careah and Kedar, he may have never met Yeshua. He said to himself, *Yeshua has made life worth living to the fullest.*

*I have a beautiful dedicated wife, and two special kids. I have a responsible life time job, and respected by most of the people. What else could a person want?*

He felt someone present, and looking around, he saw two smiling faces.

He asked, "How long have you two been here?"

Flash, smiling, said, "About an hour."

Kedar said, "No, it was like two hours."

La'no remarked, "Don't you know you can't kid a kidder?"

La'no looked at his watch. "We are a little late. Before we go, did you leave your Lazar guns home?"

Both answered yes.

Flash said, "We can take my Courser. It's parked here by your office."

Entering the Garden of Gethsemane, they saw Yeshua about 300 yards in the distance praying. It was close to an hour when Yeshua went and talked with His disciples. Then He went away from them again. As He was praying His body began to quiver, then it happened: demons charged at Him like wild dogs; others came at Him like roaring lions with teeth gashing at Him. Other demons jumped at Him like wild oxen with huge horns trying to gouge Him. A group of them made like mad bulls snorting, hooves striking the ground, trying to crush Him. The Demons were out to kill Him before He went on the cross.

Once Yeshua got to the cross, there was no hope of them ever leaving their place of torment. Yeshua began to cry out, "My bones feel like they are out of joint, my tongue is sticking to the roof of my mouth." Then He began to sweat drops of blood. He cried out, "Father, why have you forsaken me? Father, is this the way you want me to die? If not, remove this cup, and I'm ready to go to the cross."

The disciples did not see or hear what was happening. Then the unexpected happened, a Legion of Angels appeared and chased the demons back to the pit, never to be free again. Angel Michael put his arm around Yeshua and comforted Him. He may have said to Yeshua, "I wish I could take your place, but I cannot do what you are going to do."

The Angels didn't stay very long but should have. Judas showed up with a band of men acting like mad dogs. Then he kissed Yeshua on his cheek affectionately, and the mob grabbed Him and drug Him to the worst mad men on this earth. La'no and King Flash wished they had their Lazar guns. Kedar wanted to fly at them with a vengeance.

Flash stopped him; he said, "If they grab you, they will kill you thinking you are a demon."

La'no, gritting his teeth, said, "we at this time have no other choice but get home and get all spaceships ready for takeoff. Maybe we can do something to help Yeshua later." La'no made plans in his mind to go and help Yeshua before they murdered Him.

La'no called Ken, "What is needed to get all ships ready for takeoff in less than 24-hours?"

"Each ship has a 1,000-gallon water tank being filled. We are working as fast as we can, on the water recycling system to get it working perfectly. The water desalination needs a few adjustments. We are adding a dehumidifier that pulls in any moister that is outside of the ships. Water will be our biggest problem on this trip. All human waste and most garbage will be put in plastic bags and sent to the sun for disposal.

"All animals are on board that we decided to take. There are guards at each ship to make sure each person takes one small case with their personal belongs, nothing else."

"We have six hours to start the take offs, and three hours to be in outer space. Six ships will take off every minute, I'll be the last ship to leave this planet. I don't want to watch what they are putting Yeshua through. I'll be tempted to go there and clean house."

Kedar went in to La'no's office and said, "I just came in from the outside. I heard Judas, being a priest, went into the temple and tried to give the 30 pieces of silver back, but they would not take it, so Judas threw the silver on the floor and went outside of the City of David and hung himself."

La'no flew his Courser to Jerusalem and hid his Courser behind the wall of the City of David. He went where the Pharisees were beating Yeshua; He got hot and madder than a green hornet. He was about to take his Lazar gun out when Yeshua saw him and shook His head no, and motioned His head to leave. La'no tried with hand gestures to stay and help Him, but Yeshua formed his lips and said, "No!" He wanted to kill a couple of Pharisees just for the hell of it, but turned and left, feeling sorry he could do nothing.

Kedar was there also with a large long loose robe over his head and wings. He, too, left disgusted. Instead of going home, he went to La'no's office, tears in his eyes made the grim announcement.

"The Romans put Yeshua on the cross at 9:00 this morning."

Wonder and Careah were listening what Kedar had said; both began to sob, tears flowing down their cheeks like a water fall.

"Yeshua, we love you," they said.

Leo and May stood by helplessly.

La'no came in said, "Let's go."

Won turned and looked at her home for the last time; in another hour they would start their trip to their new home. King Flash and family plus 4,000 in the Bright Star and Kedar and Careah and their family plus 4,000 were in the Blue Star. Eli and Tara and family plus 4,000 in the Gold Star; Rush and his new wife Cayo were in the Rose Star. Rayco and Tero were in their Silver Star. Jaydor and Bo'j were in their Twinkle Star. Ken and Liza were in the Fast Star; Greg and Sue in their Blond Star. Bil and Clem were in their Police Star. Kenz and Mar'ee are in their Sweet Star.

Admirral Lenz was invited to go with La'no. Jimco and all the other spaceships were ready and waiting for the word GO.

La'no and Wonder were in their Emerald Star, sitting behind the wall of the City of David. In front of them was the temple, and they could see Yeshua on the Cross. La'no called Flash. "It's 3:00 p.m., start countdown by 10s to 60. When you get to 60, take off; the others will follow. I will take off at 6:00 p.m. sharp. My brother Leo and his wife May are with us; we will catch you before you get to the little star. I'll keep in touch with you."

Without any warning, suddenly it got pitch dark.

"Take off now, and good luck, Flash."

In three hours, it would be daylight, and he would start the camera and the x-ray camera to see what happened to the rock at the base of the cross when God the Father takes Yeshua's life. He told Moses He would kill Aaron the High Priest if He reviled any part of his lower body, even his ankles when going into the Most Holy Place to make a sacrifice. Since Yeshua is our High Priest on the cross, His lower body was exposed. The Father had no other choice but to keep His promise and take His only Son's life! When the Father would throw His wrath on our High Priest, would the Cross take the force of God's wrath? Yeshua told La'no there would be an earthquake when He would be on the cross. He forgot to ask what time the earthquake would take place.

It was a long three hour wait, suddenly at 6:00, it got daylight.

Yeshua looked up to heaven crying out loud, "My God, My God, why have you forsaken Me?"

Someone at the temple cried out, "The veil is ripped in half."

La'no knew the veil was 20 feet wide, 30 feet high, and four inches thick and held up with a 30-ton stone that came crashing to the floor. All of what was happening was being televised through the space ship. Wonder and May were crying their hearts out. The robots were checking the compartment where the animals were, making sure they were ready for take-off. Something jogged his memory, the words kept going through his head: "My God, My God."

Then it hit like a bolt of lighting. Yeshua's Father turned from looking at His Son because He had to kill his own Son. For the first time from eternity passed to this point their fellowship was never broken. Teary eyed, La'no said to himself, *How can a Father who loves His Son take His life?*

Wonder heard one of the other men on a cross ask Yeshua, "Will you remember me when you get to your Kingdom?"

Yeshua pretended He did not hear him. He wanted the one making the request to know why and what he was asking for. The other man next to Yeshua was Gestas. He said, "If you are the one you say you, are save us."

Dismas asked earnestly, "Yeshua, please, will you remember me when you get to your Kingdom?"

Yeshua turned and looked at the one making the request said, "Dismas today you will be with me in Paradise." It was close to 6:00 p.m. The soldiers broke the two thieve legs. When they came to Yeshua he was already dead. It must of have made the soldier mad, he took his spear and thrust in Yeshua's left side. At that moment, a mega earthquake valiantly shook all of Israel, Hi-Why-O was no more. The two volcanos sank into the earth. It split the huge pock the crosses were on, making a crack, Yeshua's blood ran down the crack. La'no's x-ray camera showed four angels taking the Mercy Seat out of a large stone casing and placing it so Yeshua's blood ran on the right side of the Mercy Seat.

La'no said to his wife, "Now I know for sure we are saved by His shed blood."

If His blood didn't go on the Mercy Seat Yeshua would have died in vain.

He saw the Ark of the Covenant still in the stone case that measured 14 feet wide, 18 feet long, and six feet high with a six-inch solid thick lid. The table of shew bread and the Menorah, with other temple vessels were there.

Before taking off, he watched people taking all three off of the crosses and take the crosses to the garbage dump and burned. He wanted to stay until Yeshua arose from the place he would be buried in. He gave into temptation and waited until Yeshua was buried. He saw people taking Yeshua to a huge stone with a hole cut in it with two shelfs in it. The people wrapped his body with four-inch wide linen, 100 feet long, with Frankincense and Myrrh mixed with other compounds, spread around the body into a cocoon glued to the surface of the lower shelf he laid on. It hardened like steel. Mar'ee placed a cloth over his face. The Pharisees and their cohorts wanted Roman soldiers to guard the tomb. They set the watch: four soldiers East, four West, four South, and four North making sure no one could steal the body, and they bolted the stone in the opening of the tomb.

La'no said, "That's it, we are getting out of here."

Once they left earth's gravity, they cruised at four Gs. Five was the limit. The bobot took over the space ship controls.

Traveling close 10 billion miles, the robot awoke La'no. The other two robots were standing at the door of his room. La'no realized something was wrong; the space ship wasn't moving.

He asked, "What is the trouble?"

The robot answered with a question.

"Will you come, to the control room, sir? We were not programed for what is in front of us."

Entering the control room, looking in the monitors made the hair on the back of his neck stand out. He wished he had left with the other spaceships. This was no nightmare—he wished it was. He had no idea what to do. Maybe if he shut his eyes, it wouldn't be there after opening them. *Okay, smart guy, start thinking what to do?*

He asked the robots to get everyone that handled Lazar pistols and the Atomic Blasters and every nuclear weapon on board.

The robot said, "There are 1,600 alien space ships all small."

As long as the force shield was down they could not use artillery.

A scrambled voice came through the speakers. Not a word was audile, then the word English came out loud and clear.

La'no grabbed the mike and yelled, "English."

"Doa yous speaka English?" was the question.

La'no responded "Yes, and Jewish."

"Wea no speaka Jewish, justa somea de English."

La'no asked, "What do you people want?"

"Wea likea comea anda talka."

La'no asked, "What do you want to talk about?"

"Wea needa imformatiom about a people fara awaya."

"You mean information," corrected La'no. "Okay, you can come aboard, if you have all of your spacecrafts face away from us, then we will beam you aboard. If that's okay with you."

"That fine with me, but may I bring another person with me, my good friend," replied the stranger.

La'no said, "It depends who the other person is."

"Well if you have to know, it's my wife," replied the stranger. La'no noticed his English was getting better.

"Yes, by all means, she is welcome also," replied La'no. La'no asked one of the robots to get his wife, his brother, and his brother's wife.

La'no gave orders to the robots lift the shield and get ready to beam the strangers on board.

"Have your Lazar pistols ready if they try anything funny," he added.

The strangers were beamed aboard. La'no asked their names.

"We are the Zets. I am Cordo, and this is my wife Kalo."

La'no turned and said, "We are the Bels, my name is La'no, my wife Wonder. And my brother Leo and his wife May."

Wonder said, "If you do not mind, lunch is ready, then you can talk whatever you want to say to each other."

The Zets marveled over food they never had and kept watching the Robots. Leo was watching the Zets watching the robots.

He informed the Zets, "They are mechanical machines called robots. They are programed to work, think, reason, and obey humans."

"Would you sell us one? We have gold or precious stones."

La'no replied, "We cannot sell our robots, they are like family. I will do this: I will give you a set of blue prints, then you can build your own." Then La'no asked, "Where are you heading, home or to a new planet."

"We are going to this planet. This is a picture of it; it looks very peaceful and a perfect place to live."

Seeing the picture of the planet, La'no about swallow his tongue. It was a picture of the earth they just left. La'no showed the picture to Wonder, putting a finger to his lips. Then to Leo and May, then the same thing, his finger to his lips. Giving the picture back, he said, "If I were you, I would not go there to live."

"Why not?" asked Cordo.

La'no out of habit turned a recorder on and said, "I will explain. We left there three days ago. What I'm going to tell you is the truth, Cordo. More than three million people had to cross over a river at flood stage. The river was more than one-forth mile wide. An evil Army was after them to make them slaves. They were boxed in, nowhere to go. A man named Moses held up his hands and stop the water from flowing, the river bed was dry for over a mile. The people crossed over; Moses crossed last. Then the stupid Army entered the dry river bed, when all of the Army was in the dry bed, Moses drop his hands to his side, the water rushed over them, they all drowned.

"One man named Sampson killed 1,000 soldiers with a jaw bone of an ass, then ripped a city door down, 100 feet square, and took it to the city dump and burned it. His son is just as strong as he is. An enemy army of 185,000 came to kill, and one man killed every one of them singled handed. You may not believe this—three men forced to walk in a hot furnace of 38,000 degrees and came out alive; not a single hair was burned.

"Then I saw a man walk on water across a lake. This same man, evil people killed Him put Him in a huge hollowed out stone, then bolted the hole shut with another huge stone. Three days later, someone busted the bolts, and the man they killed was not there. More than 5,000 people saw him walking and talking with many more people.

"The evil men love fighting wars, when the war is over, they start another war. Now do you want to go there and live?"

Kalo answered without hesitation, "NO, NO."

La'no said, "Do you want to talk it over with your people? I will have one of the robots beam them over."

Cordo said, "Yes, but only my Council."

"I have to call King Flash and let him know what is going on; I should have been with him about 20 hours ago. If I know him, he will turn around and be here soon."

Wonder broke in saying, "Tara will have Eli follow King Flash."

After the Council was beamed in the Emerald Star, Wonder invited them to have lunch before setting down to discuss what they were going to do.

La'no said, "King Flash will be here soon, and I think another friend will be right behind him, I'll turn the recorder on, and your council can listen to what I talk about. Cordo, you and I can hunt for another planet if you and your people want a different one. Do your people have food to eat."

"No, we expected to be on the Earth you came from."

"When King Flash and Eli get here, we will beam food to them." La'no asked, "Where did you come from?"

"We came from the Planet Liptor."

Wonder inquired, "Have you always lived there? What I mean, your ancestors, did they always live there?"

"No, actually, they came from the planet Earth in the sixth or seventh century. People were mean and hateful because we are Mulattos."

Wonder smiled and said, "You are just one shade darker than the Aquatic people. I guarantee you, no one here will never say a derogatory word against your people, and I mean never. I wish I had some of your color."

Tara came in and heard what was said, she replied, "I think your people are one of the most beautiful people God ever created."

Wonder said, "By the way when did you get here?"

"We followed Flash in a few minutes ago."

La'no said, "I'm puzzled. How did you get here from Earth?"

Flash and Eli came in, and Cordo was asked, "How did their ancestors get from the earth to here?"

Cordo replied, "I looked at your map of the Earth, and they lived where Auranitis is. They were far advanced than the rest of the World. Our technology is what got us here. They had a 100-foot high wall, more than 60 miles around the vast complex. They had modern factories of every kind to build Space Vehicles, later called ships."

Wonder asked, "Why did you leave Earth?"

Cordo smiled said, "If you have all day… No, just kidding. Most of the people became godless. You heard of Jeremiah; they treated him as a wild animal, even put him in a well. They began to torture other helpless people. One of our prophets said we must get out of there; there was going to be a mega earthquake. This place would be no more. All of our people entered every spaceship and left the earth. This happened when Ezekiel was a young priest. The people never saw a rocket ship before. Didn't know what was taking place. Our prophet was right. They witnessed the earth open up, and their Complex sank in to the earth. Not even a sign there had been a complex ever existed."

"Cordo, the planet next to ours has water, grass, trees, and clean air. At the far end of the Milky Way, there is a mega star Epsilon Aurigae, the size of eight billion Earth suns. Even though it is one billion light years away. If it explodes, no more galaxies."

"We will give you some animals to start an animal population," Cordo replied. "There will be no vote; we will take the planet. Your people are too kind. We will never repay you."

La'no broke in, "We did not do this for a reward. It is a blessing we can do his for you. So do not take this blessing from us by saying you want to repay us. Your friendship is worth more than all the gold there is. You know, Cordo, maybe someday we will need help, and you might help us, by golly." *(Not knowing in the future the favor would be paid).*

A robot came to La'no and gave him a coded message from King Flash. La'no said to Cordo, "My friend King Flash is being beamed over, then we can beam food to your people, and I know Eli is beamed behind him, then we shall all eat. Our robots are very good cooks."

Cordo said, "May I ask you a question. Who is this King Flash? Is he over you or is he from another planet?"

"He and I lived on the same planet. He and his people are aquatic people; they live where there is water, lots of water. They plant different crops, and we plant different crops, and of course, we sell to each other. He rules his people, and I lead my people. This keeps us a strong united nation."

A-see, the head robot, called from the bridge, "the Blue Star is 14 minutes away."

La'no ordered A-see to call the Blue Star and find who was leading the other ships to their new home. Without hesitation, Kedar said, "Rush is leading the other spaceships to our new home."

Wonder sang out, "Glory to Glory, Cordo and Kalo, are in for a big surprise of your life! I would not miss this for all tea in the world, and I love tea."

Tara asked, "What time are they going to get here?"

A-see said, "In 22-and-one-half minutes."

La'no asked A-see to see how close they were to a planet. A-see looked at a map showing part of the Milky Way. A-see calculated traveling at four Gs, they could be at the nearest planet in two hours. A-see said there was no way of knowing if the planet was habited or not. La'no took a vote, should they go or not. It was 100 percent to go.

After everyone was beamed to their spaceships and ready for takeoff, the Blue Star was two minutes away. The Bright Star was the first to take off. Then the Green Star, then the Emerald Star. Then the Blue Star followed the convoy. All of Zets crafts were in the air and out of sight in minutes.

King Flash spotted a large flat plateau large enough to accommodate the whole company of spaceships and Zets' crafts with plenty of space left.

The Green Star was the first to land; Tara ran to get Kalo and waited for the Blue Star, which landed last. After the Blue Star stopped, the ramp steps came down, and Tara grabbed Kalo's hand, heading up the steps, and had her ready to see something she never saw before. Her mouth dropped, not believing what was in front of her.

Tara introduced her to Kedar and Careah, saying, "These two are some of my best friends. Their people behind them all have wings and light in their foreheads."

Kalo, not sure what to say, asked, "Are they angels?"

Tara laughed, "No, but they are very special people."

Kalo, smiling, said, "Since you all are Tara's friend, I'm sure you will be my friends."

Tables were set up; robots brought food from the starships. After several hours of eating and enjoying each other's company, La'no and Admiral Lenz, who were traveling together as an advisor, motioned King Flash and Kedar to come to their table.

When they got there, Flash said, "I saw it also."

Kedar inquired, "Saw what?"

Eli walked over to their table to see what was going on. They asked him if he saw anything strange in the sky?

"Yeah, I saw a bird on the horizon."

La'no suggested they call Cordo over and see if he saw anything in the sky. When Cordo got to their table, they asked if he saw a strange craft in the sky. He shocked them all, "I saw several Zo-ites Crafts circling on the horizon, the last 15 minutes, probably checking if we are staying here. They live on the planet Zingal, four billion miles from the one we left. Most of them are 10- to 15-feet tall. Their lifestyle is far different from ours. Their diet is snakes, rats, skunks, and human flesh.

"When they kill humans by the hundreds, they have a feast lasting for weeks. They are the reason we left our planet Liptor. By luck, we met you good people."

La'no replied, "It was not luck you found us. The Lord and Yeshua brought you to us for a reason."

Flash said to La'no, "Are you thinking what I'm thinking?"

Kedar responded, "I know what you are thinking, and I'm for it."

Eli remarked, "Wveryone must be psychic! I'm for it, too. We will have to check after landing."

La'no made a motion to see if it is large enough for everyone.

Admiral Lenz responded to their comments, instead of just talking about it.

"You guys are not using your heads; the Lord or Yeshua would not have sent us to a planet that would be smaller than what we would need. You are putting your trust in what you think. Cordo, we all are asking you and your people to come with us to the planet the Lord gave us. We will be stronger to protect ourselves in case an enemy came against us."

"Admiral, we will gladly go with you to your new Planet Birth."

The council gave Cordo three cheers for naming the planet Birth, and they unanimously agreed the new planet will be called, "Planet Birth," that is close to the center of the Milky Way.

Cordo looked at every member of the council asked, "Who is this Lord and Yeshua?"

They all agreed Kedar was the best to tell Cordo about the Lord and Yeshua. Kedar suggested Cordo get his wife Kalo and their people to gather at the tables and put up speakers, that way he could speak to them all at one time."

"Good idea, good idea," responded the Admiral. Eli was elected to introduce Kedar. Careah was at his side to fill in when he forgot something important or interesting. They got on a make-shift podium. He told how they met Yeshua then started with the birth of Yeshua being born in the House of the Most High. He and Careah had them all on the edge of their seats, taking every word in as if it was their last meal. Getting close where Yeshua was put on the cross the, A-see called La'no to let him know his rocket was minutes away. He jumped in his Courser and flew into space to be ready for it. The robot B-see got the computer programed to pull the rocket to the Courser. The people below were holding their breath and cheered as the rocket entered the Courser. After landing, La'no motioned Kedar to finish, and Kedar said, "Evil men beat and nailed Yeshua on a cross to die. Careah and I are going to have La'no share the good news. I hope it's good news he just received from Mar'ee."

La'no got on the podium all got quiet, even the wind died down. La'no began, "I got this letter from Mar'ee. Most of you do not know Mar'ee, she is a beautiful lady inside and out. She loved Yeshua more than words can tell. She watched the Romans nail him to a cross, a form of execution that no human should go through or for a person to watch, especially someone you love. He was not guilty of any crime of any kind. They put spikes in His hands, one spike in His heals. They shoved a crown of poison thorns on His head. All of this was done after they nearly beat Him to death. From the time they took Him out of the garden to the time He died, they gave Him no water or food. This innocent man was spit on, had His hair pulled out of His head, and pulled His beard out by the roots.

"Mar'ee has written here; she cried three days and three nights, saying, 'Yeshua, I love you so much, why did you let those dirty beasts do this to you?' She writes, 'on the third morning I decided to go to the tomb. Why, I do not know why. I guess I just wanted to be close to Him. I know the big heavy stone was bolted to the hole in the tomb. How was I going to place spices around His head and in His mouth?

"'When I got there, I saw the stone door was beside the tomb, and the bolts busted, not pulled out, but busted. I looked in the tomb; the cocoon was there, but it was empty, then I really began to cry. Water was running down my cheeks preventing me from seeing clearly. I saw a man who I thought was the gardener. I asked him, Sir, where did you take Yeshua's body? On His next words I nearly fainted, Mar'ee why are you crying? I am here. Oh, what joy! My heart pounded so hard, I thought it was going to leap out of my chest. I threw my arms around Him, and He said, You cannot keep Me here, I have to go to My Father, then I'll come back. Please go and tell my disciples I'll see them in Galilee.

"'Yeshua is here every day and goes back into heaven every night. He has been with me one full day, telling me what I must do and I have to write what I know about Him and, put it in a scroll. The scroll will be called the Scroll of Mary. He is going to do the same with his disciples and his brothers.

"'La'no it was a pleasure and privilege to write this for you. I am now placing it in the rocket and am ready to push the button. I love every one of you, including the Zets.'"

"Admiral Lenz, I am Kalo, my husband is Cordo."

"I know who you are, the Zets."

"Well since you know who we are, I would like to introduce you to my sister Zrte."

"Why would you want to do that for?"

Kalo replied, "you both are single."

Lenz shot back, "So are a lot of other men here."

"She would like to meet you. She is a little bashful."

"Okay, you can introduce her to me in a couple of weeks."

Kalo snapped, "You are not a very good comedian; she is here behind me. Kalo this is Admiral Lenz, Lenz this is my sister Zrte."

Lenz did a double look.

"WOW! You ae one beautiful lady, but I'm nearly twice your age."

Zrte asked, "Who's counting? Anyway, I would rather be an older man's darling than a young man's slave."

"I'm not an old man, not at 30," replied Lenz. You have to be 15 or 16."

Zrte gave him a stern look. "You're jerking my chain; I'm 19-and-a-half. Look, buster, I'm willing to fight for you."

"Okay, I surrender, with a kiss to clench our engagement, if that's okay with you?"

Zret grabbed him and planted a kiss on his lips that sent him on a trip through wonderland! Her pulling power was working.

Lenz asked, "Are you willing to become a Christian?"

She replied, "How can I become a Christian when I don't know what a Christian is?"

Lenz asked, "Did you hear La'no read?"

"Mar'ees letter? Yes, I personally think Yeshua was foolish taking a beating like he did and then letting the Romans put those big spikes in his hands and heals."

Lenz said, "He did that for us, so we will not have to pay for our sins. All we have to do is believe He did it, and let Him accept us into His Kingdom. You know, Zrte, those who do not believe He is the Son of God will go to a place called Hell, where there is nothing but fire and brimstone."

Zrte asked, "Where is this Hell?"

His answer didn't faze her at first. "The unbeliever steps into Hell one micro second at death because of a Christ-less life. If an unbeliever dies anywhere in the universe, they are guaranteed a free trip through the Gates of Hell."

Zrte inhaled deeply then exhaled. "Believe me, sugar, I do not want to go there. I will trust Yeshua to be my savior," replied Zrte.

Lenz looked into her beautiful jade eyes and said, "Okay, we will have our first date when we get to our new home."

She replied, "That's what you think? I'm going to follow you like I'm your shadow until we leave here?"

Lenz said, "Shadows do disappear."

She came back at him with a smile, "Not this one."

Cordo called La'no, pointed to the western horizon sky.

Cordo said, "They were there about eight minutes circling watching to see where our weak spot is. They look but do not see, and they hear but do not listen; that is their weak points. They will not attack now, we are too many. History means nothing to them: their mistakes are overlooked. The horror and chaos they create is their way of life. They have never been defeated."

Kedar asked, "Do you mean there are other people in the universe?"

"Yes, and you do not want to meet them."

"We have God who can tramp on their whole nation as if they were a bug."

La'no called all the leaders of each starship for a quick meeting.

"How soon can you all be ready to take off?"

Cordo said, "We have everything packed, so we are ready now. The other leaders said, if everyone helps to load, we can be ready in an hour or less."

La'no replied, "Let's make it less. We have a lot to do when we get to our new home… plant fields, build homes, put up factories, get the Armed Forces to start training, most of all build a warning system. I think the Zets can help us on that.

"A-see, how long will it take us to get to our planet?"

A-see asked, "At what speed do you want to travel, four or five Gs?"

La'no said, "I wish we could do six Gs."

A-see replied, "You can, if the turbines or jets can take that speed, it will take close 12 hours."

"Do you know if the Zets can keep up with us?" La'no asked.

Cordo happened to be close by. He laughed and said, "I do not want to sound like I'm bragging, but would you believe at the speed of light."

La'no's face reddened, and he said, "Cordo, I'm sorry. I didn't mean that as an insult. Since you can do that speed, do you know where Planet Birth is in the Milky Way?"

"We can be there in a couple of hours. You said it is a billion light years from Epsilon Aurigae?"

"Yes, we are to the left of it."

La'no supplied Cordo with all the information he needed to get there. There are three oceans and three continent; you choose the one you want. If there is lots of water on any one of them, that one is for King Flash, and I'll take the remaining one. If I remember, they are about equal. I don't have to tell you what to do when you get there, do I?

"Remember we will be as one nation under God. Cordo, will you send me a radio message when you get there?"

"I can't, and will not do that, buddy."

La'no got a little hot asked, "Why not?"

"We fly faster than radio waves. I think I said some time ago we travel at the speed of light. We were working on factor speed, and new heat shields. We had to stop because of the Zo-ites. They out number us nine-to-one. Their air ship flies only at the speed of sound. I'm thanking my lucky stars we fly at the speed of light. If they come after us, it will take them at least two years at the speed they fly."

La'no replied, "I'm sorry I underestimated you. I was going to ask you a lot of questions. I see there is no need. I know for sure you will handle everything that is to be done."

As Cordo was leaving he said, "We will be on our way in 45 minutes."

La'no said, "I'll say goodbye now; I have to do a lot to attend to. Oh, oh, what about your daughter Zrte, will she be going with you?"

"Good question," responded Cordo.

La'no smiled, saying, "If she has her mind on Lenz, she may stay with us."

"La'no, I'm glad to hear that. If I made her to go with us, she would bug me all the way to Birth."

"Lenz doesn't show his emotions, but I know for sure, if she went with you, he would be hard to live with. Hey, wait a minute! Why don't he go with you? No, I'm sorry he's needed here."

"That is okay, Zrte will be thrilled to be close to Lenz. Maybe Wonder will teach her to cook some of that good food you have been feeding us."

"I'm sure she will.

"Have you named your continent? King Flash said he and his people named theirs Continent Aqueous, if they get land with a lot of water. Cities will be named Lake, River, Creek, Pond, Stream, and so on."

La'no replied, "He and the Shepherds voted yesterday. Our continent will be the United Cities of Amcarta. Each city will be named after trees and fruit trees, Cherry, Peach, Plum, Apple, Ash, and so on."

Cordo said, "We named our Continent Zodiac, and each city will be its sign. Aries, Cancer, Leo, and planets."

King Flash called La'no, "Cordo is on his way. I wished him and his people God's speed."

"Thanks Flash, are you all ready to take off? I want you to go first. Have your robot call if it detects anything alien. I know you can out-fly the Zo-ites. I'm very serious, Flash, I do not want to lose a friend. I'm going to tell you, only you a big secret.

"Ke'no and his Navy friends have been drawing plans for a new type of gun they named Angry Hornet. I looked the plans over; I'm sure hope it works. The Super Jets will have four rotary guns, two front, two aft. Each gun will fire 25 rounds a second. That is 3,000 a minute. The nose of the shell is hollow and filed with TNT. The range of the bullets are accurate at the distance of one mile. The gun turret moves back and forth, bullets spread 100 yards each way. The TNT filled bullet hits the target, blows it a hundred feet in all directions. I said, Angry Hornet, you are one stinging gun."

Flash replied, "We are going to make that Angry Hornet sting like a nest of mad hornets, so we will."

La'no smiled and said, "You're right, Flash, as soon as we are set up, we are going to build this hornet's nest."

Flash was going to his space ship. He suddenly turned and said, "Our Super Jets fly at the speed of 5,000 miles an hour. we can't have them go any faster; they will shoot themselves down."

La'no came back at him saying, "Not if we can make the bullets fly faster."

Flash laughed, "I'll see you when you get home."

Everything was built that was to be built. Even the Planet Birth seemed to enjoy having the people being there. It was early morning, and Wonder could not get out of bed; her body was cold, but she said she was hot. Doctor Janes was called, and after examining her, as she left the room, she motion La'no to follow her.

She said to La'no, "I'm terribly sorry, but there is nothing I can do."

La'no's voice trembling, "What do you mean there is nothing you can do? You are a doctor—that's what you do, you help people get well."

"La'no, she was bitten by a bug that had the black plague, known as the bubonic plague, probably before you got here. There is no cure."

"No, no, I said no! She is not going to die."

"La'no, she has a week to a month at the most," replied the doctor.

"That's what you think, Doctor. I have a doctor that can heal her in an instant."

"Cordo, I need your help desperately! I mean, please, Cordo," La'no was crying and sobbing so hard, he was hard to understand. Cordo knew there was something desperately wrong. He got in his fastest ship and was at La'no home in a few seconds. He walked in without knocking and saw La'no on his knees sobbing.

La'no looked up at Cordo, tears flowing down his cheeks.

"Cordo, can you get my wife and me to Jerusalem in less than a week?"

Cordo said, "I can do better than that. We are in luck; we have developed the factor speed. How does this sound: seven times the speed of light! Why? What happened?"

"My wife got the Bubonic plague. She is sealed in a clear plastic box with an air tube and a filter. The plague is very contagious."

Cordo replied, "I have no idea what the plague is, but I think we better get moving."

The earth was in sight; Lano asked Cordo, "Do you know where Israel is?"

He said, "No, you have to guide me to it. If you feel up to it, you can take control of this ship and fly there."

"Okay, it's getting dark. I'll know the way to Galilee. His home is there. I will not have to hide to get to His house, I'll land right in His front yard. People will not be out in the streets, at night. We can carry Wonder into the house."

Approaching Galilee, Yeshua's house was easy to find. It had a small date tree close to a window. La'no landed without a sound, or so he thought. A man came out of the house, and He said, " La'no, what brings you here?"

He replied, "Wonder is very sick, and I need Yeshua to heal her."

Peter said, "I'm sorry, but He is no longer here. He is in heaven with His Father."

La'no fell to his knees, crying so hard his breath was beginning to leave in jerks.

Peter said, "My wife and I are visiting His mother. Carry Wonder into the house."

Getting the Plastic case into the house, Mary asked, "What in the world is this?"

Peter replied, "Wonder is very sick."

Mary asked, "Why is she in that thing?"

La'no said, "Mary, my wife has a very contagious disease. She has only a few days to live. I hoped Yeshua would be here to heal her. I can't think straight; I don't want to live without her. I'm sorry I bothered you Mary. Cordo and I will take her home, and I don't care to talk about, I mean, I don't know what I'm going to do. Thanks for your time Mary."

When they were about to leave, Mar'ee entered the room.

"Hey La'no, what are you doing so far away from your new home?" She saw tears in his eyes, then the case Wonder was in. "What happened? Why is my friend Wonder in that thing?"

Looking at Peter, she said, "Please help her."

Peter lifted the plastic case off of Wonder and took her by her hand, and Wonder sat up and said, "Peter how did you get here in Cherry?"

La'no fell to his knees weeping like he never did before. He looked at Peter and said, "I will give you anything you want, I mean anything, Peter."

Cordo, teary-eyed, was speechless and dumbfounded. He never witnessed a healing in his life time.

Peter said to La'no, "I did not heal Wonder. My Lord did it. You have to know that." Wonder looked around asked, "What's going on? Why are we here?"

Back on Birth in Cherry, the bad news of Wonder hit hard, Tera the most. She said, "Won does not have the Black plague, or whatever."

King Flash's wife, Adorable, could not believe Won was near death.

Kedar and Careah both got the bad news that Won had a few days to live.

Kedar remarked, "Naw, she isn't sick; she can't be. I talked with her yesterday; nothing was wrong then. Everything was fine."

Ke'no and his sister Te'ro were trying to comfort each other. Most of their country was in shock.

It was getting close to daylight; they had to leave before people saw them and caused trouble for having dealings with demons.

Cordo said, "No use sending a message we will fly faster than the message."

Peter asked them for a favor, "In a few months, I must go to Mesopotamia, my ministry is there."

Cordo joyfully said, "Give the date, I will take you there, maybe by then I may have developed Factor 8."

"Okay, how about six months from this day?"

"I'll be here, you can count on it."

On the way home, La'no said, "Cordo, I will pay you for what you have done for us."

Cordo replied back; his voice was a different tone, "I never get angry with a friend, I don't want to start now. I know this trip is worth a lot to you, I can never repay you for what you did for me."

Getting back to Cherry, people were dressed for a funeral. La'no left Wonder leave the ship first. You had to be there: words can never say what happened when Wonder appeared at the door of the ship. After a few moments of shock, Wonder got a standing ovation and cheers that no movie star ever got.

Their country was stronger than any other. If the Zo-ites tried to fight a war with their prepared country, they wouldn't have a chance, like a snow ball in a hot oven. Anyway, it would take the Zo-ites more than two years to get there. Twenty-five Angry Hornets would love to show their stingers.

Rayco has an announcement to make. He and Te'ro are getting married.
Jaydor said, "Bo'j and I are going to make it a double wedding."
Kenz and Mar'ee announced, "Why not make it three?"
Admiral Lenz came forward: "I have one of the most beautiful ladies God has ever created for me to marry, and you all know her name is Zerte daughter of Cordo and Kalo.

CPSIA information can be obtained
at www.ICGtesting.com
Printed in the USA
BVHW040348110520
578778BV00006B/54